IRAQ
+
100

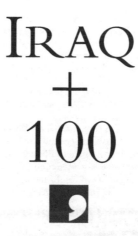

Stories from a century
after the invasion

Edited by
Hassan Blasim

With additional editorial support from
Noor Hemani & Ra Page

First published in Great Britain in 2016 by Comma Press.
www.commapress.co.uk

The opinions of the authors and editors are not necessarily those of the publisher.
A CIP catalogue record of this book is available from the British Library.

ISBN   1905583664
ISBN-13   978 1905583669

This book has been selected to receive English PEN's PEN Promotes and PEN
Translates Awards, supported by Bloomberg and Arts Council England as part of the
Writers in Translation programme. English PEN exists to promote literature and its
understanding, uphold writers' freedoms around the world, campaign against the
persecution and imprisonment of writers for stating their views, and promote the
friendly co-operation of writers and free exchange of ideas. www.englishpen.org

This book has also been supported by a grant from the British Institute for the Study
of Iraq.

The publisher gratefully acknowledges assistance from Arts Council England.

Set in Bembo 11/13 by David Eckersall
Printed and bound in England by TJ International Ltd.

Contents

CONTENTS

Foreword

THE IDEA OF THIS book was born in late 2013 amid the chaos and destruction left by the US and British occupation of Iraq – chaos that would drag Iraq into further destruction through Islamic State control over many parts of the country.

No nation in modern times has suffered as much as Iraqis have suffered. Iraq has not tasted peace, freedom or stability since the first British invasion of the country in 1914. Since then, Iraqis have lived through a long saga of wars, death, destruction, population displacement, imprisonment, torture, ruin and tragedies. So, perhaps unsurprisingly, it was difficult to persuade many Iraqi writers to write stories set in the future when they were already so busy writing about the cruelty, horror and shock of the present, or trying to delve into the past to reread Iraq's former nightmares and glories. In the process, I personally wrote to most of the writers assembled here in an attempt to encourage them to write for the project. I told them that writing about the future would give them space to breathe outside the narrow confines of today's reality, and that writers needed more space to explore and develop certain ideas and concepts through story-telling. I said they would be writing about a life that is almost unknown, without relying directly on their own experience or their personal reading of the past or the present. Writing about the future can be wonderful and exciting – an opportunity to understand ourselves, our hopes and our fears by breaking the shackles of time. It's as if you're dreaming about the destiny of man!

At first, I was uneasy that we would pull it off. The idea had originally been suggested by my friend and publisher, Ra Page, along the lines of 'imagine Iraq a hundred years after the US occupation through short fiction'. My unease arose from two sources – the first was related to Iraqi literary writing in general and the second to the literary scene and my personal relationship with it.

In an article that dealt with the beginnings of our project, the journalist Mustafa Najjar wrote, 'The reluctance of Arab writers to address the future has long been a great mystery, at least to me. The walls of repression and censorship that confine Arab creativity so severely offer in themselves an ideal environment for writing about the future, a space that is free of the taboos that weigh on the past and the present.'[1]

Iraqi literature suffers from a dire shortage of science fiction writing and I am close to certain that this book of short stories is the first of its kind, in theme and in form, in the corpus of modern Iraqi literature. Faced with the fact that Iraqi literature lacks science fiction writing, we have tried in this project to open more windows for Iraqi writers. We asked them to write a short story about an Iraqi city 100 years after the start of the occupation and said they were not required to write science fiction but had complete freedom to choose any genre of writing that could address the future. We did not select specific writers to take part in the project: we opened the door to anyone who wanted to take part and to imagine an Iraqi city in a hundred years, whether academics, novelists, or writers of short stories.

There are many possible reasons for this dearth of science fiction writing in Iraqi literature, and in Arabic literature in general. Perhaps the most obvious reason is that science fiction in the West was allowed to track the development of actual science from about the middle of the 19th century onwards. The same period was hardly a time of technological growth for Iraqis, languishing under Georgian 'Mamluk' then returning Ottoman overlords; indeed some would say the sun set on Iraqi science centuries before – as it set on their cultural and creative impulses – in the wake of the Abbasid caliphate. What have the subsequent rulers and invaders of Iraq done since then, the cynic might ask, apart from extol the glorious past when Baghdad was the centre of light and global knowledge? Knowledge, science and philosophy have all but been extinguished in Baghdad, by the long litany of invaders that have descended on Mesopotamia and destroyed its treasures. In 1258, the Mongol warlord Hulagu set fire to the great library of Baghdad, a place known as The House of Wisdom, where al-Khwarizmi had invented algebra, Sind ibn Ali had invented the decimal point, and Ya'qub ibn Tariq had first calculated the radius of Earth, and the other known planets. The library was burnt to the ground. Precious books on philosophy, science, society, and literature were deliberately destroyed. Those that weren't burnt were thrown into the Tigris and the Euphrates by the invaders. The water in the Euphrates is said to have turned blue from all the ink that bled into it from the books. From the Mongol Hulagu to the American Hulagu, George W., this once great seat of learning has been destroyed and pulverised. Bush the butcher, and his partner Blair, killed hundreds of thousands in Iraq, and in the process its museums were once again ransacked. All this without mercy or even shame, and in full view of the free world. But let's leave aside Mr Bush, Mr Blair and the other killers still on the loose, and go back to our modest project, which tries to imagine a Modern Iraq that has somehow recovered from the West's brutal invasion, in a way that Iraq didn't recover from the Mongol one, in the blink of an eye that is 100 years. Our project tries to imagine the future for this country where writing, law, religion, art and agriculture were born, a country that has also produced some of the greatest real-life tragedies in modern times.

It is my belief that it is not only science fiction that is missing in modern Iraqi and Arab literature. I share with colleagues the view that Arab literature in general lacks diversity when it comes to genre writing – by which I mean detective novels, fantasy, science fiction, horror and so on – just as there is little diversity or transparency in our day-to-day lives. We, by which I mean Arabs today, are subservient to form and to narrow-minded thinking because we have been dominated by religious discourse and by repressive practices over long periods, often by dictatorships that served the capitalist West well, bowing to its whims and fitting with its preconceptions. But certainly that does not mean that science fiction is entirely absent from the Arab or Iraqi literary tradition. Reference is often made to the Arab roots and origins of science fiction and fantasy in *A Thousand and One Nights* and in *Hayy ibn Yaqdhan,* the thought experiment novel written in the 12th century by Ibn Tufail. Some people trace it to the Sumerians even further back, as the Iraqi writer Adnan al-Mubarak has done on several occasions. Al-Mubarak says, 'Modern science fiction is strongly associated with the scientific-technological revolution and usually focuses on related issues. On the other hand science fiction is a literature that is part of a very old tradition that goes back to humanity's first ideas about the real world and about the potential for human beings to constantly explore nature and the world. As is well-known, we find the first written material about journeys, including to other planets, in Sumerian literature (*The Epic of Gilgamesh*, for example), and in Assyrian and Egyptian literature. In an Egyptian text written four thousand years ago, we read about imaginary journeys to other planets. It is important in this context to go back to al-Mubarak's essay, 'How the Sumerians invented space aeronautics'.[2] In the middle of the last century Arabic writers, from several Arab countries, started to experiment with writing science fiction and fantasy, and Egyptian literature was the dominant presence. But those short stories can be criticised for their references to the supernatural, to spirits, devils and fairytales that all fall back on that all-too dependable myth-kitty, *A Thousand and One Nights*. *Hayy ibn Yaqzan*, on the other hand, met the conditions for writing science fiction in an interesting way, and I believe that modern Arab literature has not paid enough attention to that work, just as it has not shown enough respect for the treasures of Sumerian, Ancient Egyptian or Babylonian writing.

Inflexible religious discourse has stifled the Arab imagination, and pride in the Arab poetic tradition has weakened the force and freedom of narration, while invaders and occupiers have shattered the peace that provided a home for the imagination.

The picture is not wholly bleak however.

Today there is great hope in a new generation, a generation native to the internet and to globalisation. It is a generation that is open-minded, more adventurous about genres, and more impatient to exercise the freedom to express oneself and to experiment. Serious attempts to write science fiction and fantasy have started to appear, especially now that the science is so much easier to get hold of: the internet gives us access to research, to documentaries, and to other novels and books from around the world, and allows us to follow the extraordinary and rapid development of human imagination through science and other forms of knowledge.

As for my second, more personal source of unease about editing this anthology, this arose from the fact that I am a writer whose work found its place in the wider, non-Arab world while I remained on the margins of the Iraqi literary scene — a scene I have always chosen to keep my distance from. Iraqi literature is populated by 'official' writers who belong to the Writers' Union and other cultural institutions. It is a literary scene that depends on personal and cliquey relationships and on the corruption in the press and in the Ministry of Culture. Literary and other cultural projects in Iraq usually come about through personal relationships that are not entirely innocent. Being out in the cold like this comes with its disadvantages, and I have often pressed my editor, Ra Page, to write to Iraqi writers directly and asked him to make some of the selection decisions: if I were the only person in the picture and the sole decision-maker in this project, it might irritate or surprise some Iraqi writers, who are more accustomed to literary projects initiated by people from within the narrow circle of 'usual suspects'.

The stories collected here have been written by Iraqis from various generations, and display a variety of styles. The authors were born and grew up in a variety of cities; some have abandoned those cities seeking peace and freedom in exile, while others have chosen to stay on and bear witness to their cities' plight to the end.

The cities featured here – Baghdad, Basra, Ramadi, Mosul, Suleymania, Najaf – are all wildly different places, in fiction and reality, but are united by the tragedy of modern Iraq – the tragedy of a people that is desperate for just a solitary draught of peace. As Iraqis, at home and abroad, we are desperate for this peace, and thirsty for the imagination and creativity essential to rebuild this ancient country – this land of the two rivers.

Hassan Blasim, September 2016
Translated by Jonathan Wright.

Notes

1. 'Arab Fiction Faces Up to the Future', Mustafa Najjar, *Asarq al-Awsat*, 9 Nov 2014.
2. 'How the Sumerians invented space aeronautics', Adnan al-Mubarak, available in Arabic on www.iraqstory.com, and in English at https://thecommapressblog.wordpress.com.

Kahramana

Anoud

THE DAY KAHRAMANA WAS to be wed to Mullah Hashish, she stabbed him in the right eye and ran to the American Annex of Sulaymania.

The local media of the Islamic Empire of Wadi Hashish had not yet caught up on the matter. While the rest of the world was using holographics (because maintaining fiber optic cables across Water War zones had proved impossible), Wadi Hashish considered anything but paper newspapers printed on metal-presses to be western blasphemy. Plus the people of Wadi Hashish were never in a hurry.

By the time Kahramana had snuck out of the last Wadi Hashish checkpoint, *Akhbar Al Imara (News of the Empire)* had just ran this on their front page:

> Oh what a joyous day of jubilation. Allahu Akbar! The Islamic State of Wadi Hashish today wears its festive green and black ribbons on every streetlamp. Civil servants have been ordered by the great, the brave lion, the sword of Allah, Amir Mullah Hashish – May Allah reward him in abundance – to cook giant pots of lamb stew at every intersection to feed the poor, as a gesture of his generosity, on the day he is to wed the most beautiful woman in the Empire (according to our sisters, as the virtuous Amir – May Allah reward him in

abundance – has never laid eyes on a woman before), no other than our blue-eyed sister, Kahramana. The grand wedding reception for men will be held in the courtyard outside Wadi Hashish Municipality tomorrow at sunset. Attendance is mandatory.

'Eat shit!' said Lieutenant Abdulhadi as he tossed the newspaper aside and rubbed its ink off his fingers. NATO in Baghdadistan were the biggest consumers of *Akhbar Al Imara*. They had no idea what happened up north, he thought. Baghdadistan analysts just gobbled up every word those metal printers spat out. It was the only way they could know what Mullah Hashish was up to since he never went digital. The Lieutenant had been sent to the Islamic Empire border under NATO orders. He missed the sandy, sunny, humid climate of Port Basra and hated the bone-dry freezing wind up in this place. Ever since NATO had hit the Empire with its sterility gas, it had snowed all year across the northwest side of Iraq, all the way to the Mediterranean. The sterility germs hadn't worked, because the Hashishans were still breeding like cockroaches, only now in six feet of snow.

At the end of his shift, the Lieutenant climbed into his trailer, dropped onto his bed, kicked off his knee-length boots and sat there, rotating the stiffness out of his ankles. He was staring through the window and letting out deep puffs from a cigarette he'd confiscated, when gradually he realised he was looking at a woman tangled up in the barbed wire.

'What now, goddamn it!'

He climbed into his boots again, grabbed his machine gun and coat, and walked out towards her.

'Go back, get back,' Abdulhadi waved at the woman. 'No Nations Union League trailers here. Go away!' But she stayed put until he was an arm-stretch away – then she revealed her face. Her skin was like marble and she had plump red lips and the nose of a television star. Her face was lightly dotted with pink freckles. Her most prominent features, however, were her dark-blue eyes. They sent a shiver through Abdulhadi colder than the frostbite in his ink-stained fingers. A strand of her bluish-black hair snuck out of her headscarf and twirled in the breeze. Kahramana was the most beautiful woman Lieutenant Abdulhadi had ever seen. He had also never seen blue eyes before. 'I beg you, brother,' she interrupted his stare, 'they will kill me.' Her eyes were welling up now. Mesmerized by her, Abdulhadi clicked back the safety on his firearm, turned his back to her and gestured with his hand for her to go.

Kahramana walked for another day and a half until she saw the blue flag of the NUL. There, she was strip-searched, de-liced, and sub-categorized by posture, teeth, size, skin colour, and finally by age before queuing up for finger-printing, DNA registering, and to have her head shaved. She wept for her long hair. In all her 16 years, this was her very first haircut.

But the bald head only made Kahramana's eyes stand out more. They were so prominent that all the women in the female quarters avoided her and started to spin stories about how she would use witchcraft to win over the soldiers and NUL officials.

They were right. How else could you explain why Kahramana started to be picked again and again by the NUL, to represent migrants at the strategic emergency workshops? Her face was featured in all NUL emergency appeal broadcasts since she arrived at the camp.

But the women especially despised Kahramana because her pleading eyes appeared on a giant NUL billboard at the entrance of the camp. Her deep blue irises were the size of truck tires, staring down at everyone who entered the camp.

The Americans, however, were accustomed to all shades of blue eyes, and Kahramana didn't move them. Her rape-asylum case took three years of multiple rejections and appeals before any ruling was made.

During this time, Kahramana was examined by two of the three medical and psychological committees: the first chaired by the New York-based Acts For Humanity to determine if Kahramana displayed the appropriate psychological symptoms of a rape victim (they let everyone pass!); the second committee consisted of migrant doctors from the camp, operating under guidance of NUL doctors in NYC, to do a virginity test. The third and final stage would have been a face-to-face interview at the Annex, an hour's drive from the camp, to determine whether the sex was consensual or indeed forced, upon which the woman would be granted rape-asylum status. But since Kahramana had gouged Mullah Hashish's eyeball out before he'd had a chance to consummate the matrimony, the second committee decided that Kahramana was a virgin, thus could not possibly have been raped. Her case never made it to the third committee, and even then it would still have been for the US Annex of Sulaymania to make the final decision.

But Kahramana's face had not gone unnoticed. Lobby groups started to march in support of her outside the Annex perimeter, banging pots and burning flags. For months, they would gather to throw kalashes[1] at the perimeter fence, yelling 'Rape comes in all forms!', until eventually the NUL intervened and allowed Kahramana to have a face-to-face interview with a migration officer at the Annex.

The Annex's Chief Immigration Officer – a redheaded Texan who gave the ultimate 'yay' or 'nay' to any appeal – was hunched in his chair scribbling down notes on his touch-pad with his pinky. He was struggling to decode, in his broken Arabic, what Kahramana was saying until towards the end of the interview, she leaned across at him and tugged at his sleeve. She pointed at the television bolted to a wall in the interviewing room. The Texan squealed, staring at the image of the man who just happened to be on at that moment. 'Sweet Jesus, THAT was your husband!?'

Mullah Hashish was in a black frock and turban, waving a threatening index finger and yelling at his disciples standing under the pulpit: 'We will send them all to hell.'

Word got out. Kahramana was hailed as a hero. A US-Sulaymania News reporter appeared on television, standing outside the Visa Hall at the Annex border.

Reporter: A remarkable story of bravery and survival. Just 16 years old, Kahramana managed to attack and significantly wound the head of the so-called Islamic Empire after he tried to rape her. Kahramana is now undergoing psychiatric therapy and …

Anchor: Jason, is there any news on her immigration appeal? I mean surely they cannot send her back!

Reporter: The Annex government is yet to come up with a decision on that. But, as you can see behind me, there are crowds appealing [the protestors whistle and cheer] for Kahramana to be granted asylum.

Anchor: Keep us updated. Thank you, Jason.

Reporter: Absolutely.

Two days later, *Akhbar Al Imara* ran this on the front page with a title in red ink – which was remarkable because they only ever used black or, on religious occasions, green for their headlines.

The great, the brave lion, the sword of Allah, Amir Mullah Hashish – May Allah reward him in abundance – has vowed to cut off the head of Kahramana, the serpent corrupting our pure sisters and brothers with her filth, after the Amir Mullah Hashish – May Allah reward him in abundance – discovered that Kahramana was not the pure virgin she pretended to be. Kahramana confessed to the Amir – May Allah reward him in abundance – that she had committed filthy acts of adultery with no less than 12 other men and 3 women

5

who will all be beheaded in the courtyard outside Wadi Hashish Municipality tomorrow at sunset. Attendance is mandatory.

On top of this was a grainy photo of men and women in shackles and red overalls on their knees, looking miserable, with four men in black hoodies labeled with a green 'anarchy' sign made of two crossing machetes. They were brandishing their vintage (and no-doubt broken) AK–47s at the camera, grinning.

A week later the women's rights group *Kuchan Sulemani* hijacked the Annex's armoured truck carrying thousands of copies of *Akhbar Al Imara*. They loaded the newspapers into their van and sped off, having taken the driver out with a sedative dart. The *Kuchan Sulemani* activists then appeared at the Annex's main border gate, the following dawn, to erect a large papier mâché art instillation made of thousands of copies of *Akhbar Al Imara*, just in front of the Visa Hall. Plastered across every surface of the installation was the front page of *Akhbar Al Imara,* as well as large print-offs of the three women accused of having sex with Kahramana. Each face was the size of a car's front windshield. Another print-off, of Kahramana's face as it appeared in so many NUL publications, was also plastered on it, along with a Sorani Kurdish phrase hailing her a feminist icon. The activists were tear-gassed away a few hours later, along with the local press who had shown up to cover the story.

Kahramana stared at the sight of her face appearing sporadically across the new items on the TV screen bolted to the wall of the restaurant. She was fascinated by all the attention she was getting. There she was, eating well up on the eighth floor of Freedom Fires Tower, with the Women's Rights' Attaché from the American Annex of Sulaymania. The attaché had come to congratulate Kahramana on winning her appeal to stay in Sulaymania. She was also there to discuss Kahramana's nomination for the Courageous Women's Award.

The attaché gently touched Kahramana's arm, telling her how much she sympathized with her ordeal. The Iraqi interpreter mechanically touched her other arm as she translated.

Kahramana bowed her head and said nothing. She was contemplating the matter while sipping her soda. Only she knew that on that day, retiring to her master's chamber early and dressed in only the most tantalizing of undergarments, she had caught Mullah Hashish, pants around his ankles, with another man. The other man hiked up his pants and bolted, leaving Mullah Hashish to fall to his knees with his face in his hands.

She knew that Mullah Hashish would never let his secret out. He, who called homosexuality a 'foul western concept' and ruled that all homosexuals should be 'eaten alive by wolves' – he would stop at nothing to keep her from spilling this secret. He was going to kill her.

Kahramana looked at the interpreter. The interpreter looked at the attaché. Kahramana leaned forward and, copying her, all three women huddled so close their heads almost touched. Kahramana began to tell them how, on the night of her wedding, she caught Mullah Hashish forcing himself on another woman. The woman was crying for help so Kahramana attacked Mullah Hashish and freed the woman. They both ran for the border but the other woman did not make it. 'What happened to the other woman?' asked the attaché. 'She was eaten by wolves,' said Kahramana.

Anchor: Jason, remarkable news that Kahramana has finally been granted asylum and she's been nominated for this prestigious award! Tell us what's going on over there.

Reporter: Well, as you can see, the crowd behind me here – they have gathered to celebrate Kahramana receiving the Courageous Women's Award and for her finally being granted asylum. It has been a long struggle, a long road to this victory. I have with me here Sherein Agha, chair of the NGO, Kuchan Sulemani, who has long fought for Kahramana's case and other women like her.

[The camera moves to put both Sherein and Jason in the frame.]

Reporter: So you must be very proud of today's success. Tell us your thoughts about these announcements and what they mean.

Sherein: 'Well yes clearly we're very glad at how things turned out for Kahramana; she's a brave woman and it's been a remarkable journey. But she is only one of tens of thousands of... our figures estimated at least 120,000 women... who are at the mercy of men like Mullah Hashish in the so-called 'Empire'. Men who think it is acceptable to murder and rape women and to perform genital mutilation on young girls. This battle is far from over and...' [Sherein raises both hands to gesture hopelessness.]

Anchor: Jason, I have to cut you and Miss Agha short there. Thank you very much.

A week later *Akhbar Al Imara* posted a photo of the now officially one-eyed Mullah Hashish in his signature black frock and turban. This time, and for the first time, he was surrounded by six pregnant women standing sideways, three to his left and three to his right so that their huge bellies could be seen, despite the flowing black garments they wore covering everything but their eyes. Mullah Hashish was standing in the middle pointing his index finger threateningly as per. Underneath a caption read: 'We will outnumber them and send them all to hell.'

The news story read:

'By order of the great, the brave lion, the sword of Allah, Amir Mullah Hashish– May Allah reward him in abundance – all women must be either pregnant or breastfeeding at all times. Men must follow the example of the great steed with his many wives and marry as many women as they can afford. All men must have a minimum of three wives as an expression of commitment to populate the glorious empire and outnumber the enemy. Men whose wives are not pregnant or breastfeeding will be called in for questioning, counselling and medical assessment. When called, attendance is mandatory.'

But in NATO-run Baghdadistan, few were worried. In fact, the day *Akhbar Al Imara* ran their story, NATO officials could be seen in cafes all over the city, reading their copies and twitching with joy. They had finally figured out the sterility gas weapon thing, or so they thought. Jason was chasing that story, as he did last time.

Kahramana put the stained newspaper down to give her full attention to the tall and handsome Central Annex Intelligence officer who had come to question her one more time about what she knew of the mysterious Mullah Hashish. Kahramana was excited to see that he had blue eyes just like her. She pointed to her eyes then at his, nodding and smiling at the interpreter. The dull and puffy-faced interpreter looked at the CAI offer: 'You got that?' 'Yup,' he replied without looking up, scribbling away with his pinky on his pad.

It was another long and boring interview, and it turned out this CAI officer was almost as dumb as Mullah Hashish. He kept asking her the same questions over and over. Now and then Kahramana secretly snuck glances sideways at the crowds gathering in the snow, far below, like ants behind the giant T-walls. They were waiting to get onto the Sulaymania side – the sunny side. One after the other, their visas would be rejected, Kahramana thought. She smirked at the stupid CAI officer. But he didn't notice, he was too busy poking holes in her story.

A week later Kahramana was detained for giving false evidence. Her deportation was scheduled for a fortnight after the interview with the blue-eyed intelligence officer.

Kuchan Sulemani activists half-heartily hanged their pots and burned Annex flags for Kahramana. But this time media didn't even show up. They were too busy filming the nationalist flag-heads swinging bricks at the NUL headquarters in Erbil and chanting for the deportation of all Arab refugees. The paparazzi re-tweeted an alleged sex tape of Kahramana which the flag-heads circulated from an earlier meme that Wadi Hashish had used to show Kahramana was not a virgin.

The NUL took Kahramana back to the camp and stalled her deportation for a further six months, trying to delay the inevitable. Kahramana cried and cried until her eyes turned black and her hair started showing grey and her face wrinkled. Then came deportation day.

The NUL drove a dozen female refugees to the West Gate, and parked up just beyond the perimeter fence, on the far side of the T-wall. There they handed out survival kits (water bottles and energy bars mainly), and dignity kits (tampons, HIV and pregnancy tests), to each woman, as well as leaflets explaining their rights as refugees and how they could appeal the decision in five years time.

Dragging her feet between the T-wall and barbed-wire fence, Kahramana suddenly saw Abdulhadi. He was still working as a border patrol. She tried to reach out to him but by now she was on the wrong side of the wire. She called to him: 'Help me brother! They're going to decapitate me!' To which Abdulhadi responded with a brief, blank stare before returning to his job of waving official vehicles in and out of the gate. It wasn't that Abdulhadi didn't recognize her. It was just that he had other things on his mind: scrounging migrants, the low quality of confiscated cigarettes, this damn NATO-induced snow.

Note
1. Kalashes: handmade Kurdish shoes.

The Gardens of Babylon

Hassan Blasim

Translated by Jonathan Wright

To Adnan Mubarak

ONE OF THE TIGER-DROIDS has been tampered with. The public garden system has only just launched the model, and some nine-year-old boy has already hacked it, making it circle pointlessly in the air, above everyone's heads. Visitors have begun gathering round, laughing at it, including me. We watch as a supervisor intervenes, along with a male and a female droid, and together they coax the thing back down to earth. As the crowd disperses, the supervisor issues the boy's mother with a fine. There's nothing unusual about this kid's hacking skills, of course: Babylon is now a paradise for digital technology developers, a playground for hackers, virus architects and software artists.

It's still too early for the queen to arrive, so I watch the children having fun with the crocodiles in the water tank. There are other animals, originating from every continent, roaming freely among the visitors: tame, friendly beasts, from birds to insects, as well as smart-trees, developed to match the rhythm of this 'Age of Peace and Dreams' – as our queen likes to call it. And our queen is right. I don't understand the people who object to her policies. This virtual life, with so much affluence and creativity, really is the true rhythm of the age. It means there's extraordinary harmony between our imaginations and our realities. It was the federal ruler of Mesopotamia who gave the director of the city the title 'queen'. I think she deserves the title. I don't know, maybe I'm wrong, but she's a strong woman and she's left her mark on our city by building it on the principles of creative freedom. We have built peace and prosperity through imagination. That's what the queen says, and today she's going to open the Story-Games Centre, which recently recruited me. The queen took over the management of Babylon ten years ago. She divided the city into twenty-four giant domes. At first HK Corporation objected to this division, but the Chinese later did a u-turn, saying they hadn't initially understood the queen's plans. Of course, they only said this after the queen gave them the contract for managing the city's water provisions. Maybe what I'm saying today about Babylon's imagination policy doesn't exactly apply to me, since these days I find it difficult to work. But for most citizens it's perfect. My problem is I need to relax too much. And it's like my imagination has run dry. I have to finish my first story-game this week, but I'm too laid back. Creativity requires a certain exuberance. I have no ideas, no images; too often I feel bored and empty.

On the screen above the Gardens, I watch an advert for the new water trains that will soon come into service. These are fast trains that will supply the city with water from central and northern Europe. I feel an overwhelming desire to leave the Gardens and head for the abandoned Old City, but I've left my facemask at home. Our queen has now appeared on the screen, with the CEO of HK, and they are drinking glasses of water with the new train behind them – the pride of Iranian industry. Over recent years these water trains have become a key factor in the selection of city managers. City managers are appointed by the Governor General of Federal Mesopotamia, with the proviso that the international companies that manage the provinces endorse the choice. Things have gone well with the water trains. For several years, Babylon had faced the prospect of going thirsty. Then the Water Rebels had formed and started to agitate against the Chinese company. The Water Rebels are constantly on the move and are still active in both the abandoned city and in the new domes. The rebels still don't like the way the water is being apportioned. HK Corp distributes the water from a central point and armoured, automated trucks are responsible for supplying every house with its quota of water. To some extent, I can see why the Water Rebels are angry; some people hardly seem to have enough e-credit to pay for their quota, while in rich areas you see special trucks filling swimming pools and fountains with the stuff. Several times the rebels have hacked into the trucks' software and made them dispense water in the poor parts of town. What I don't understand is why they reject any dialogue at all with our queen.

I'm hungry. I message the restaurant and they send me the nearest waiter-bot. I like this restaurant. They've designed their robot waiter to look like a cook and also like the first astronaut to set foot on the Moon. He's very funny. Everything you order comes out of his belly. I credit him on my phone for the sandwich and the orange juice and, as I eat, I re-read a classical text by a writer who lived here at the beginning of the previous century. It's quite a boring story about violence in the age of oil and religious extremism. I was disappointed when I was offered the job in the Archive Department. My dream was to work in the New Games, designing my own story lines. But they assigned me the task of converting the old stories by our city's writers into smart-games. The manager said it was one of the most important departments. 'You will have the chance to open the door for the new generation to discover the distant past of Babylon.' Of course the manager is exaggerating, because who's interested in that bloody past today? Most young people only follow the best-selling space story games. The garden is teeming with visitors. It's obviously because the queen's expected to visit. There are visitors from all over the world, although today most of them are Chinese. They and their families look very happy. Why not, since it was they who designed the new domes, and they who are running Babylon? Almost everything – the transport system, energy, the hospitals, and smart-schools. Not to mention the food and water business. No one can deny the ingenuity of the giant domes. Each district is a circular space like a giant sports ground, roofed over with a smart glass dome that absorbs the sunlight, which is the main source of energy in Babylon. All the districts are linked by amazing underground trains. The Chinese have also given the inhabitants of Babylon the privilege of Chinese citizenship, so we Babylonians can go and live in China as if it's our own country, and likewise for Chinese people wanting to live in Mesopotamia. I call up my dear Indian friend Sara. Her phone isn't available. I can't read any more. The rhythm of the story makes me feel sleepy. I switch the story to listening mode in the hope that the reader's voice will inspire me and give me an idea about how to design the story-game I have to produce.

The doorbell rings. I look out of the window. The morning sun floods the trees in the garden. The oranges shine like my mother's golden earrings. How I miss her! I miss her kisses, her tears and the way she sighs at life's ups and downs. I miss her earrings, the golden love hearts my father bought in Istanbul in the 1970s as a honeymoon present. That was when my father played the oud and my mother was a history teacher.

The doorbell rings again. A large flock of sparrows is pecking the grass in the garden. My father waves from beyond the garden wall. Frightened, the sparrows fly off to the neighbours' garden.

'Good morning, father. All well? Has something happened?' I say as I undo the padlock on the door's steel chain.

'Nothing, son, nothing, I just wanted to see you.' He shakes my hand and wipes the sweat from the end of his nose. He looks into my

eyes and embraces me. He's carrying a black bag, which he waves at me.

'Mr Translator, I've brought you a present,' he says.

'A present in a black bag, Lord preserve us. What is it, father? Not a Kalashnikov, I hope.'

'War won't end as long as there are people, my boy, war after war. When was the world without wars anyway? My God, to hell with it,' Father says as he comes in.

I get breakfast ready: tea, eggs and cheese.

My father lights a cigarette after swallowing one bite of egg. He picks up his teacup and looks around at the pictures hanging on the wall. He stops in front of a copy of a painting by Fayeq Hassan, *Horses in a Desert*.

'What news of your English stories?' he asks as he looks at the picture.

I take his present out of the black bag. It's an explosive detection device that looks like a wand. He takes it from me and explains how it works, pretending the table is a car. My father's worried I might be targeted by Islamist groups because of my new job. They might see translating American literature as treason and a form of cooperation with the occupier. In fact, the wand turns out to be just a plastic stick with the end connected to a mirror to check underneath cars. In recent years the killers have developed new ways of reaping people's souls. They stick explosive devices under people's cars. It doesn't matter who the person targeted is. What matters is that the constant mayhem should serve their objectives. The explosive devices either kill you instantly or blow your legs off, in which case your neighbours, relatives and friends will say, 'Well you should praise God and thank Him for ensuring you survived!' Then you'd be a legless man who praises and thanks God. Violence sculpts you and in this case turns you into half a statue. Violence is the most brutal sculptor mankind has ever produced. A barbaric sculptor: no one wants to learn lessons from the works he has carved. I graduated from the Languages Faculty a year ago. I studied English. I was lucky to get a job in the foreign literature magazine. The magazine specialised in translating literature from various languages. While I was studying I translated one story by

Hemingway and another by Margaret Atwood. I had them published on the culture page in Awraq magazine and my translations apparently caught the eye of the editor-in-chief. He contacted me when I was about to graduate and asked me to visit him at the magazine after I graduated. I had signed a contract with the foreign literature magazine within three weeks. The people at the magazine chose a Raymond Carver story for me. I hadn't read anything by him, but I had come across the name Carver in a critical article about dirty realism and about Carver's writer friend, Richard Ford.

My father poured himself another cup of tea and went out to the garden.

I watched him from the window. He sat at the table under the orange tree and stared at the table as if he were looking at himself in a mirror.

Every ten years my father changes into another person. It's as if he dances faithfully to every new rhythm in our shitty country, turning with each new turn. My mother's brother, who translated Freud's books, used to call him 'the chameleon'. For the past few years he's kept repeating that it was the chameleon that killed his sister. My mother died suddenly of a heart attack. We were three boys and a girl. My mother disembarked from the ship of our life and we had to battle the stormy and unpredictable waves of life with my father. Before we were born, in the 1970s, my father was obsessed with communism and playing the oud. He used to hold communist parties just for his comrades and play them revolutionary songs. There was a well-known song at the time called Lenin in Baghdad. At the beginning of the 80s my father abandoned communism, volunteered in the army and became a sniper. He won several awards for bravery in war. As a sniper, he was skilled at making neat little holes in the skulls of Iranian soldiers. In the 90s my father deserted, but was caught and spent his days in one military prison after another. He treated the prisons as mosques: he started to pray and grew religious. Instead of thinking about a world full of free and happy people, he started thinking about a divine roadmap that led to Heaven or Hell. When the dictator was overthrown at the beginning of the new millennium no one understood him any longer. He would descend into strange periods of seclusion.

He would disappear for a week or more, then suddenly reappear. He wouldn't let anyone ask why he had disappeared. He became introverted and depressed. After the U.S. forces left the archaeological site in Babylon, my father got a job as a guard in the antiquities department. Some time in his first days at work, he declared, 'The American infidels have turned the site of the oldest civilisation in the world into a camp for stupid soldiers, occupying a country in the name of democracy.'

I take the lift to the tenth floor. At the door to the main dome the info-bot reminds me of the security procedures for going out into the abandoned city. I pay him and borrow a facemask. The door opens and then closes behind me. Dust blocks out the sun. Sandstorms are blowing all over the city. I turn on the mask's vision screen and walk up to a dead fountain more than a hundred years old and sit on the rim. Three drunks are messing around on the street corner. Sara's phone is still unavailable. She must be busy with the customers at the pleasure hotel. One of the drunks goes down on his knees theatrically while the other two imitate executing him. I think they're making fun of the country's murderous past – Daesh and the sectarianism that was fed by oil money. This abandoned city is now just a desiccated relic of a bloody past, a past that was steeped in religious fanaticism and dominated by classical capitalism. The violence only stopped after Babylon was engulfed by the effects of climate change and the oil wells had practically run dry. How puzzling and painful is the march of man! The rivers and fields dried up. The desert advanced and obliterated the city. At the time, the federal government was struggling to mobilise modern technology to stop people abandoning the city forever. The federal government took advantage of oil exports in the final years, started some big investment projects and opened up to the world. For many third world countries the decisive factors in shifting the balance were that clean energy matured and spread all over the world, people in the West rose up against the brutal and selfish capitalist system and the idea of one destiny and one world without hypocrisy or selfishness gained strength. People started saying, 'This is neither your country nor my country. It is our land,' and this was not just a slogan. People agitated and started to take the initiative to change the world through intelligence, humanity, and real justice. In the middle of the century the name 'Iraq' was changed to 'Federal Mesopotamia'. First the Germans built technically advanced districts in Babylon and other cities, which made it possible for the residents to live with the desert storms. The sandstorms had made life in the city miserable by making the air unbreathable. During the time of the German districts, generations developed that were skilled at digital technology, until the Chinese appeared on the scene and stunned the world with the domes concept, which is now seen as the ideal solution for cities that are subject to desertification and environmental degradation. After the Chinese domes were built Babylon's 'Magical Generation' was born – a generation that now exports the cleverest software and the most extraordinary scientific discoveries to the world. Thanks to our queen, the domes have become the new gardens of Babylon. Each dome in Babylon has its own special character. One dome is known for its fascinating cybergardens, another for its digital arts centres, and a third for its space dreams, such as the ninth district, where they are now building the world's tenth space lift. If it wasn't for the Water Rebels, we would be living in complete peace. I understand why the rebels object to the water allocations but violence is an emotional and primitive solution in a situation that calls for self-control and reflection. I don't know what solutions they are proposing. Blind rage is an inhuman weapon. It's a form of selfishness and hollow pride. I'm reminded of our city's classical writer, who was angry at how bloody and violent life was in the city at the turn of the century. Okay, why not? That might work as the intro to his story-game. Why can't the story-game be inspired by how the writer ended up? He took refuge in Finland after Islamic State took over his city. In Finland he wrote four collections of stories and a play, then he disappeared until they found he had killed himself under a tree in the forests of northern Finland. The temperature was 40 below zero, and when I looked for his date of birth, it turned out he was born in summer, in the month of July. Maybe he was born when the temperature was 40 above zero. Maybe he was born in the sun and the fact that he died in the snow could be written into the start of the game. There could be two options for the player: a sun icon or a snow icon. If the player clicks on the sun icon the game begins at the birth of the writer and then we move on to his story, but if they choose the snow icon the player starts with his suicide under a tree with a pistol in his hand. Or the way into the game could be just two numbers: -40 or +40 and the story would have two tunnels and the player would choose. Shit, what a dumb idea! I'll go for a little walk and maybe get these superficial ideas out of my head, and maybe inspiration will descend on me. It's not my day! Near the old parliament, there's a teacher wearing a facemask and a group of children who look like primitive animals in their masks. It's clearly an educational tour of the past. Some Nigerian tourists go warily into the ruins of the parliament building, taking photographs. I taste a bitterness in my mouth. I go back to the dome and get aboard a driverless, automated taxi and go to the pleasure hotel where Sara works. Most tourists prefer taxis with local drivers they can chat with. In the pleasure hotel I take the lift to the fantasy floor. I submit a blood sample to the analysis-bot, and he opens the door. I pay twenty e-credits and another door opens into the hall where the really sexy women are. I choose a beautiful Turkish girl and have sex with her in the zero-gravity room. I go down to the cybersex floor where Sara works. As soon as she sees me she rushes to hug me.

'What floor were you on?' she asks with a smile.

I tell her about the Turkish girl and she slaps me on the ass. 'You idiot!' she says. 'On the romance floor there's a new girl from Basra that would make your head spin if you saw her.'

I hug her again and whisper close to her lips: 'I've missed the way you think.'

She pushes me away gently and taps me on the head with her fist. 'Let's leave now, you story prick. What's up with you? Are you okay?'

I tell her in brief about my problem making a story-game out of the text by that writer who killed himself. She pulls me by the hand and says cheerfully, 'Let's go to the Selfish Gene bar, it's a vintage bar and it might do your classical text some good.'

In the bar, Sara orders a beer from the alcohol machine and I have a new arak they started making two months ago. We take a seat in the corner. From the screen on the table, Sara chooses the privacy option. A glass cocoon surrounds us. From the screen I choose a new Swedish song that Sara likes. I ask her how her mother is in India. 'My mother's resigned from the Mars project,' she says. 'She's taken issue with the recent constitution written by the One World committee. She objects to the part that says that every citizen in space must undertake never to rebel against Martian government through violence. You know the debate — it's been raging for more than seventy years. A simple argument: if a violent rebellion took place and any parts of the settlement were damaged, it could mean all the settlers die. Life is still fragile there and it can't tolerate any violence. My mother objects and says it lays the basis for a space dictatorship. Anyway, you tell me now, what's your story problem?'

I don't like the taste of the new arak. Sara fetches me another drink made in South Africa that I haven't drunk before. It tastes sharp and pleasant. I look into Sara's big eyes and say, 'My dear friend, quite simply, I'm a short story artist and I want to write my own story-games and novel-games. I don't get any joy from turning classical literature into smart games. Quite honestly, their stories don't excite me very much. Besides, there's nothing new in the story of the writer who killed himself. I think it's one of his weakest stories. It was the last story he wrote and then he committed suicide.' Sara suggests I take the Games Centre by surprise by turning an almost dead classical story into an original, advanced story. Then they will trust me and give me a chance to move to the department that composes new story-games. Sara takes from her pocket a small metal box and puts it on the table. She opens the box, which looks empty. 'Here's the key. With this you'll finish the story within a day!' she says.

'No, please Sara. You know I don't like psychedelic insects. Maybe smoking something natural, okay. But I don't approve of electronic parasites.'

'Life is short. You have to try an insect at least once,' Sara replies. 'Believe me, it's one of a kind. It was developed in Brazil and now it's colonising the whole world. You can't take it by youself. You have to take it with a partner you trust and who trusts you, so that they can keep the thing under control. It's your partner who decides when your trip ends. Don't worry and don't be so serious. You trust me, right?' Sara uses her phone as a magnifying glass and looks into the box. She wets the tip of her finger and puts it in the box, and the microscopic insect sticks to it. She puts her finger into my hair and sets the insect free. 'Calm down, it's not working yet,' she says. 'The insect needs to find the right place on your scalp first, you numbskull. And it won't start to take effect until I activate it from my switch. I'll send the app for neutralising it to your phone. Some people can stop the effect of the insect during the trip by themselves, like someone who's asleep and realises they're dreaming and they have to wake up. But not everyone manages that. The important thing is you have to relax. I'll monitor the insect's progress and your brain activity and stop it when the time is right.'

The next morning I decide to go to Dome 7. From there, I can go on to the abandoned city and then to the old site of the ruins, where the lion of Babylon used to stand – the lion that was moved to Dome 14 with other important antiquities some years ago. Together with Sara's insect, being at the site of the lion might stimulate my imagination. I take a facemask and some food and water. I re-read that old writer's story and leave.

It's just desert. I locate the site of the lion through the e-map on the screen of the mask. There are lots of sandstorms and a hot wind. I send Sara a message: 'Activate your insect.'

'Have a good trip, story prick,' she replies.

I try to find the site of the old oil pipeline. Five minutes pass without me feeling anything. Maybe my brain is too tough for the insect to penetrate. I feel uneasy in this deserted place. I can hear children's voices. I climb a sandy hill. I think the oil pipeline lies beyond it. At the base of the hill, on the other side, I see a group of children playing football. How can they play without facemasks? I approach them and the referee, a young man, waves at me as if we're friends. A thin boy scores a goal after the defender tries to block him. They start arguing and the defender head-butts the boy who scored. The forward's nose starts to bleed. The match stops. Next minute, the forward is back home and his mother is trying to stop the bleeding with cotton wool while telling him off for playing rough. She stuffs his nose with cotton wool and asks him to hold his head up high. I know this boy. It's the writer who killed himself, but when he was a boy. I go out to the family's back garden to check up on this. Yes. Definitely. This is the pomegranate tree he was born under in July. His mother is now screaming in front of me, and carries on screaming until the woman next door climbs over the garden wall and helps her with the delivery. Where is he now? Okay, he's on the roof of the house. He's sitting among dozens of red birds. He throws seeds to the birds and takes a book out of a large wooden bird tower. He has installed a small shelf of books inside this tower. He might be hiding the books from his family. What's he reading? Ah, *Demian* by Hermann Hesse. Suddenly the sandstorms die down. Thick snow falls in what's now a vast forest. I see smoke rising. I head towards it. It's a small wooden hut with a sauna close by. The smoke is rising from the latter. A naked man comes to the door of the sauna smoking and drinking alcohol. Who else could it be! It's the old writer in flesh and blood. A white beard and a bald head and a glum look on his face. Although he's no more than forty years old, time has cruelly scarred the features of his face. I like this Finnish forest. I walk away from the sauna and go deep into the darkness of it. I spot a wolf. I'd better go back to the writer's house. The author sits in front of the computer, writing and drinking alcohol and smoking, wearing a green hat. Suddenly he gets up and slams the computer against the edge of the table and finally kicks the wreckage of the computer like a goalkeeper kicking the ball upfield. He goes into the kitchen, takes a psychedelic mushroom out of a drawer, eats some of it and sits at the table smoking. I sit opposite him. He puts his hat on the table in front of him and in turn I take off my facemask and put it on the table. Minutes pass as we stare at each other. 'What do you want from me?' he asks. I'm not sure whether he's addressing me, because maybe he's under the influence of the mushrooms and can see someone else, or maybe he's talking to the characters in one of his stories. In the corner of the kitchen there's a wand for detecting explosives. He might have made it himself to recreate the ambiance in one of his stories. The wand is the father's gift to his son, the translator. How pathetic he is. He seems to have a gloomy imagination and his creative resources are very simple. He gets up and comes over to me. He puts his hand on my shoulder. What's happening surely isn't for real. He's hallucinating! He speaks to me, or rather he tells his story, which I know by heart. I don't pay him any attention. My mind wanders to a black cat lying under a delicious sun. I can feel it breathing. I feel as though I'm settling down inside the cat. I merge with the cat, while our writer goes on telling his story:

After my father went out to the garden, I picked up the teapot and followed him. I asked him if he wanted any more tea. He didn't answer, then started to talk about how wonderful orange trees are. 'Did you know, my son, that orange trees spread across the world from ancient China, where the orange was the king of foods and medicines. What a splendid tree it is! It flowers and bears fruit at the same time.'

'Father, are you all right?'

My father doesn't respond. He stands up and picks an orange. As he is about to speak the black cat, stretched out along the top of the garden wall, opens its eyes.

Through its eyes I can see bright sunlight flooding the scene. I can see the father sitting with his son under the orange tree. I can hear an enormous mass of sounds. I can make out every note and mutter in this feast of sounds. At first the sounds surprise me but after a while they make me uneasy. I try to ignore the concerto of sounds and concentrate on what the translator's father is saying.

'Listen to me, son. That Abu Zahra, he never listened to what I said. I warned him and pleaded with him. In my head, he became the rebellious angel. The oil pipeline explosion tore him to shreds and roasted him. It's Babylonia. It's damned. He didn't believe me. This lousy country is inhabited with devils. We're just slaves, man. Don't be an oaf. I've said that a hundred times. He ranted on about morals and conscience as if we were living in God's promised paradise. Everything he said reminded me of the Arabic religious drama serials: morals eloquently expressed in a moribund language. Abu Zahra – you know him, my colleague, a fellow antiquities guard – he blocked his ears and didn't turn his useless brain on. I swear by God Almighty, I kissed his hand and pleaded with him on his last night. We were sitting close to the Babylon lion.'

24

I leave the cat. I feel sorry about that. I felt really comfortable inside it. I sit close to the guards at the lion, wearing my facemask. They light a small fire to get warm.

'It was a cold winter's night. I buried myself in my coat and started listening to his nonsense, my blood boiling. He kept saying the same thing, like a preacher in a mosque. Shame, man. This is your country, and those people are bastards who burn and steal in the name of religion and want to take the country a thousand years backwards so that they can live in their paradise with slave girls and virgins and all that bullshit.'

I take my mask off and the guards disappear, but the lion of Babylon is still there. It's a beautiful night. The sky is clear and the weather is mild. For sure I'm in another season. Not winter and not cold, or even sandstorms. What time am I in? I hope I don't get lost. I lie down on the sand and look at the stars twinkling in the sky. I shut my eyes. The cat on top of the wall opens its eyes. I can see the father and his son the translator again. The father gets up, touches the leaves of the orange tree and continues:

'Six months ago the parliamentary committees began to descend on the archaeological area. The Antiquities and Heritage Agency accused the Oil Ministry of destroying the ruins of the city of Babylon by extending a pipeline for oil products across an archaeological area that hadn't be excavated, but the Oil Ministry denied it and said the pipeline had been built in an area where two other pipelines, one for gas and one for oil, had been in place since 1975. The Antiquities Department didn't give in but submitted the case to the courts. The department said that the ministry's pipeline would irrevocably prevent the Babylon ruins being reincluded on the list of world heritage sites after the former dictator had messed with them, because in 1988 the Iraqi authorities had carried out restoration work on the ruins but UNESCO, after inspecting the site, said the work did not meet international standards. Materials had been used that were different

from the original material used by the Babylonians, and on some pieces of stone they had carved the words 'From Nebuchadnezzar to Saddam Hussein, Babylon rises again.' So UNESCO insisted that the ruins of the city of Babylon could not be included on its list. When the media reported the story of the new pipeline, a fierce debate broke out between the political parties in parliament and they started accusing each other of corruption and serving foreign powers. My wife's uncle, who is known as Abu Aqrab, visited me and made me a tempting offer. He said his armed religious group wanted to blow up the old oil pipeline in Babylon and he asked Abu Zahra and me to help him. My wife's uncle knew Abu Zahra well. They had worked together in a primary school in the days of the former dictator. Abu Zahra taught religion and her uncle taught geography. The uncle is now a senior official in an armed religious organisation called the Sword of the Imam. The organisation claims to be fighting the new government and the infidels, and it calls everyone traitors. The organisation was set up by a cleric who had broken away from a broad-based religious movement that had laid down its weapons and joined the nascent political process. The mainstream movement changed from being a movement of murderers that fasted and prayed, into one with ministers, members of parliament, businessmen and people of influence. Within a year they and their religion and the rest of their world had drowned in the sea of corruption that swept the country. Now the Sword of the Imam was offering a large sum of money in return for us turning a blind eye to their activities during the night shift at the ruins. They would sneak in and blow up the oil pipeline, then issue a statement on YouTube saying they had blown it up as a warning against building a new pipeline in Babylon, and that the government of corruption and occupation, together with the Americans, were stealing the country's oil while the people were starving and impoverished. Oh, and death to traitors.

'I told Abu Zahra we wouldn't be helping them to kill innocent people and they could just blow up a pipeline in an area far away from any people. And besides, when it comes to this oil — we'd been living for decades in fear and terror and conflict because of this oil.

What have we seen it bring, other than death and oppression and shit? Let them blow it up and rid us of this oil and its curse forever. Eveything else had been plundered in this Babylonian site. The bones of the ancients and the liquidised bones of prehistoric life had both been stolen, and what had we gained from guarding the greatest civilization in the world? We were guards protecting thieves. In the time of that bastard the dictator, the president's cousins had dug up antiquities and sold them to the West, as part of its ongoing collection of antiquities and oil. And today, the imam's cousins want their share of this store of bones. They want to make a new deal with the smart markets of the West.

'Abu Zahra categorically rejected the offer from the Sword of the Imam group and threatened to write to the security agencies and to the governor if they didn't stop their threats. I never saw anyone so stupid in my life! Which governor and which security agency was he talking about? All the security agencies were militias that belonged to them. Abu Aqrab himself went to see Abu Zahra and threatened him. But what can I say? He blocked his ears and dug in his heels. Life's crazy. Life's shit.'

The father falls silent and stands up. He looks at me, his son now, and, hugging me, asks me to forgive him. He puts his cheek against my cheek and his tears wet my skin. He takes from his pocket a DVD wrapped in ordinary paper and puts it on the table.

'Keep it,' he says as he leaves.

The cat leaves at the same time. It goes down to the neighbours' garden, then climbs up to the second-floor window of their house. It sits on the window sill and looks at what's inside the room. There's no furniture in the room – just a red Persian carpet. A naked man, with his paunch hanging beneath him, in the prostration posture for prayer. His whole body is covered in hair. He looks just like a pile of hair. A young woman is leaning forward right behind him. She puts her middle finger up his asshole, while the man moans with pleasure. He suddenly stands up straight, then bows. He's performing Muslim prayers and every time he bows or prostrates, the young woman sticks her finger up his ass. Maybe he imagines she's one of the houris of paradise. Finally the gorilla man turns over on his back and kicks his legs in the air in ecstasy. Then he gets up and goes out. The woman sets about locking the door. I look at her beautiful slim body. It looks like Sara's intoxicating figure. Where is Sara? Why don't I get in touch with her? Does what's happening have anything to do with the story by our writer who killed himself? There's no mention of the man praying with his ass bare in his story. The ass man comes back and knocks loudly on the door. He kicks the door and starts shouting, asking the woman to open the door. The woman sits on the floor and starts crying. The cat tires of the man shouting behind the door and goes back to the garden. It prowls warily, then suddenly braces itself to pounce. Maybe there's a mouse there. I have a good look. Ah, okay, it's just a little bird.

The old writer slips a pistol out of the table drawer and goes out.

I follow him. He walks barefoot across the snow. I walk behind him. I ask him to stop but he keeps walking. I shout out loud: 'Stop. I know you. I'm a story designer like you and I've come to turn your story into a smart game!'

Our writer looks back. 'It's all the same,' he says with a smile.

The cat goes back to the house of the translator, who sees it through the window. He opens the door for it and it goes up to him. He strokes it, picks it up and carries it in his arms. He looks at the computer screen. I can't see anything. I'm outside the cat now. Where am I, I wonder? What's he reading? Maybe he's translating the Carver story. In the original story he's translating *What We Talk About When We Talk About Love*. Bloody cat! Maybe it felt me inside and evicted me. The translator plays the DVD that his father gave him. I can't see anything that's on the screen. It's true I'm outside the cat but now I'm close to the lion. Always the same places, but outside time! I don't need the cats' eyes. I know the content of the DVD. I've read the story dozens of time. The video starts, with night descending on a view of the giant oil pipeline. The only light is the light of the moon. Abu Zahra is down on his knees with his hands tied behind his back and his eyes blindfolded, next to the pipeline. The antiquities guard, the father of the man translating Carver, comes into the frame. The guard looks at his colleague Abu Zahra for some moments. He bends over him and kisses him on the head and moves out of the frame.

I feel very thirsty. The translator opens the window in the room, his hands trembling and terror in his eyes at what he's seen on the DVD. What's all this ranting and raving that goes on inside our skulls? A brutal struggle for ephemeral survival. An illusory survival, just a postponed death walking about on two legs. What is this instinct that imprisons us? Can imagination solve the riddle? The cat leaps from the window. The girl's scream reaches their neighbour. The translator runs to the neighbours' house. He bangs on the door but no one opens. He leaps from the wall to the garden, then smashes down the door to the house. I stay in the translator's room. I roam around his house. It's a modest house but neatly arranged. So this is the style of houses at the beginning of the last century. In the sitting room there's a picture on the wall that strikes me as familiar – a picture of a young girl standing under the Lion of Babylon. It's the same picture I keep in my room in Dome 2, a picture of my mother when she was a child. Perhaps it just looks like my picture. Could it really be the same picture? It is my mother. The translator saves the poor girl from the man who's praying, who broke down the door of the room and started threatening the girl with a knife. I don't understand what happened to him. A short while earlier the pious gorilla was enjoying having her finger in his asshole. I look for more pictures in the translator's house. I come across a photo album of his life. It's my history.

The camera moves to a place far from the oil pipeline. The antiquities guard blows up the pipeline by remote control. Abu Zahra burns. I burn too. I scream in terror. Darkness descends on the forest. The pain is unbearable. Someone wraps me in a blanket to smother the flames. Our classical writer fires the bullet into his head as he sits under the tree. I don't want to die. I shiver from the intense cold. I'm stretched out close to Abu Zahra as he burns. The pain in my body stops, but the smell of roast flesh makes me feel sick. The cat goes out into the street, then runs in panic towards the main road. The smell of human flesh burns my brain. I want to get rid of everything. I just want to be this cat. A police car almost runs it over. The cat cuts through the streets of the damned city of Babylon. It goes through houses, then goes down into the gardens of other houses. It climbs a tree, then walks cautiously along a branch that almost touches the balcony of one of those historic Babylonian-style houses. On the balcony there's an old woman whose face radiates goodness and wisdom, sitting in a wheelchair and watering the flowers on the balcony. 'Go to Adnan,' she whispers to a flower. 'Go to Adnan.'

Might Adnan be her son, or her dead husband? I very much enjoy the sight of the old woman and I feel a strange peace course through my feelings. The smell of Abu Zahra's flesh subsides. Peace and the smell of flowers descend. The old woman puts her lips close to the plant and whispers a song to the flower:

'From winter we learn the magic of our fable: warmth,
    nakedness, bed
From time we learn how to store memories in the
    drawers of the spirit house
From autumn we learn the shape of the leaves of life

From cruelty and hatred we learn how strange the face of
    man is
Then we scatter our thoughts
And play again...
The mangle of life as it drips saliva on the shirt of our days!
We're frightened and we gather
We fall in love and we part
We learn the game and play it!
We learn to laugh from the silence of the toy that is
    broken in the arms of man
We go to sleep and wake up
Then we go to sleep and don't wake up
It's the sleeping rock that said, 'Life is the mirror of death.'
Both of them are a dead life!
We learn fear before faith
We learn faith before love
We learn love before truth
So we make a mistake and learn to be dizzy, as if it's a
    lesson to be learned
We learn how emotion drifts from the music of silence
    and speech
From the depths of caves blows the wind of our toy that's
    broken in the lap of a child
From sleeping fields and forests blow all the stages of
    drunkenness
The forest of life a grape
The forest of death a barrel

The forest of life fermentation
The forest of death a cup
Then the fingers of man hold the wineglass of pleasure
and he eats the thorns of uncertainty
Then we inscribe our poor human sentence
On the blackboard of darkness:
'Sleeping in oblivion'.

The cat thinks about coming down from the tree. The old woman notices it. She smiles at it and calls it: 'Puss puss puss puss.' The cat advances warily along the branch and jumps onto the balcony. It sniffs the old woman's feet. The old woman puts out her fingers to the cat and it sniffs those. The smell of flowers on the old lady's fingertips puts me at ease. The old woman strokes the cat's head. I feel the affection, the love, the peace, the value of human touch and the sweet power of love.

I feel numb.
    I doze off.
    I dream.
    I wake up.

In the cyber garden of Babylon, the weather is more than wonderful. Sara lets out a shrill laugh every now and then as I tell her about my trip.

    Sara says, 'I did everything I could to control the effect of the insect so that you could have a good trip, but your brain's so stubborn and so sunk in melancholy that even that Brazilian insect wasn't any use.'

    'Okay, Sara,' says Adnan. 'What you say may be true but your Brazilian insect did me an invaluable service. Firstly, my story-game will be based on the cat as a main character for getting into the story of that writer who killed himself. But more importantly, what's really surprising about what happened is that I finally found out who my grandfather was. You might not believe it, Sara, but my grandfather was the man who translated the Carver stories.'

The Corporal

Ali Bader

Translated by Elisabeth Jaquette

THE TRUE IDENTITY *of the alleged soldier apprehended two nights ago in a café, speaking about his life and the circumstances surrounding his death, has still not been confirmed. The things he claims to have experienced are historically quite possible, as they are supported by records. News of the man has spread quickly, although there is little information available. According to the* Kut Observer, *two days ago local metropolitan police detained a strange, angry man speaking in an accent apparently dating back 100 years. This individual claims to be a soldier in the American War, who was born in 1960 in Nasiriyah, promoted to the rank of corporal, and then killed in the city of Kut in 2003. Investigators are looking into his testimony and outlandish claims. Meanwhile, the man insists that what he says is true, and will not stop repeating his tale.*

I'll tell you everything, if I can, except for the falling, from heaven to earth. My voice echoes... boom... and I'm dying all over again. I don't know what my death looks like this time, what it's like at all.

What's important is I'm someone else today, not the soldier I was a hundred years ago. I'm not scared anymore, not like I used to be. I'm intent on telling the truth, no matter the cost.

They say truth is timeless. This tale happened at a specific time, though: the time of the truth. It would be pretty grand if I told you the truth, and went into every detail.

Whatever the cost. Especially since you know I'm not alive, that I've been dead for a long time. The truth is, I'm a fallen hero. That's right, a war hero, the last soldier in the American War. You want details? I'm a fallen Iraqi hero. How's that? Well, to make a long story short: a black American sniper shot a bullet through my forehead in 2003, about a hundred years ago.

★

My name is Sobhan. I was born in 1960 in Nasiriyah, and grew up to be just an average soldier in the Iraqi army. 'Iraq's Army of Heroes' the media called it back then. I can't tell you any more about my job or the military operations I served in. That's because I was part of every heroic operation the army undertook since I enlisted, including the one where I laid down my life in Kut. I give you my word: everything I'm telling you is the honest truth. Fact, not fiction. The real truth, no deception. I can't conceal the things I've seen. There was enough nonsense in the world I lived in a hundred years ago, I don't need to add any more.

★

I joined the Iraqi army when I was eighteen. I was just a teenager back then. Tall as a ladder. Faint moustache, like a sparrow's tail feathers. Nose that stuck out like a rod. On it, a few spots like dried droppings scattered along the side of a road. I served for twenty-two years and six months. From the Iran-Iraq war in 1980 until I was killed on duty in a little battle with the American army in 2003. A minor battle, far from the main action. The war had ended two days before the day I was killed. 'Mission Accomplished.' And we'd wanted to surrender, too; hadn't wanted to enter combat in the first place. We were on that fated hilltop when their patrol took us by surprise, and when we sighted them the world turned upside down.

We heard a voice say *Halt*.

And we told them *Friends*.

But not one of them believed us. Me, I smiled at them. I turned, slightly, to reach into my pocket. My pocket, where I'd put a rose. But the American sniper sitting at the back raised his M24 rifle and fired a shot, just one shot. Boom. It hit me in the forehead. The idiot raised his weapon before I could say hi or give him the flower I'd been keeping in my pocket.

He raised his brand new, well-oiled rifle; not like the scrap metal we had for weapons. He fired a shot. Boom. Hot blood poured down my forehead.

I didn't believe it at first. Had he wounded me? I wasn't sure. I felt something hot streaming across my face. A small smile on the face of the black man in front of me. He lowered his rifle from his right eye to check whether he'd aimed well and hit his mark. A wide smile sealed the scene. And that was it.

Son of a bitch, he was good... were the last words that passed my lips. And really, they were words of admiration for the US army.

★

I started my life as an average soldier in the 3rd Commando Regiment, the one that wrought destruction dozens of times throughout Saddam's endless wars. I didn't sacrifice my life in any of his wars (Saddam's, naturally), but I was injured seven times and promoted to the rank of corporal. I received a Medal of Bravery in the Kuwait War. I joined the Air Landing Assault Regiment in Hafar al-Batin when it was reformed, after most of its soldiers were lost in battle. I made it through all those battles alive. Once during a battle east of Basra, I got shot in the ear, and something fell into my pocket. Luckily, the Iranian soldier was a poor shot. He'd aimed at my forehead but missed. Instead, his bullet hit my ear and tore it clean off. I felt blood run down my neck. I asked the doctor for my ear so he could stitch it back in place, but he couldn't find it. A few days later I felt something soft and cold in my pocket. I realised it was my ear, and shouted happily, 'I found it!'

But the doctor said, 'It's no good. It came off days ago, and it's useless now. Throw it away, bury it, or do whatever you want with it. It's not coming back.'

'What do you mean it's not coming back?'

'Mate, it's an ear, not a tyre on a car. If a couple days go by and it's not stitched back on, the veins and arteries die. That's it, what's done is done.'

So I buried it on the battlefield, while the rest of the regiment stared at me, bug-eyed, adjusting to the sight of me with my one remaining ear.

*

I wasn't ugly or repulsive with one ear; at least I didn't think so and neither did my wife. The problem was the officers, who didn't call me by my name anymore. No, they dubbed me 'Corporal One-Ear', and that's what the whole unit started calling me from then on. They took the piss out of me for that little cadaver, even though they knew it was lost in service to the nation, and not to their arses. But my ear wasn't my only casualty. There's other things I could tell you about: a piece of shrapnel ripped through my shoulder, I got another piece in my arse, and there's a third still stuck in my arm. Even with all that, I kept my sense of humor. When anyone told the littlest joke during bombings or attacks, I'd still keel over laughing.

War taught me all about laughter and levity. Even though I've got three busted ribs, none of the guts in my belly work right, and most of my teeth are about to fall out, when we were attacked we'd work through it, oil our weapons, squad attention, stand at ease, squad turn to the right in file, right turn, and on and on.

I'm telling you, my performance in combat was excellent, just as my military title suggests. Not like the other soldiers, who were no better than sheep shit. It was my job, my profession, and by choice or by force I loved it. The next unit I joined was the Republican Guard. We were known as Saddam's Guards, the Golden Division, Men of Death, Lions of the Desert, and other names that would make our enemies shit their pants if they heard we were coming for them.

I never considered killing people in war to be a crime. It was just a job, and a job that paid. A respectable one, just like any government job. It wasn't a great job, but it was an honourable thing to do for the country, for sure. I wasn't a hired killer, burglar, or thief; I was a soldier. A corporal, in fact. Part of the Iraqi army. I was just like all the other soldiers. We weren't allowed to question our orders for a mission, not allowed to ask anything, retreat, flee, oppose, or grow weak. We were there under orders: the military commanders' orders, the section officers' orders, the party's orders. And there was no discussion when it came to that, none at all. We were assigned to units, we killed, we attacked, we occupied, we earned medals, and we boasted that we were part of the Iraqi national army. That was it. I don't think the black soldier who fired the shot, hit me in the forehead, and smiled, was any different to me when it came to that. He wasn't allowed to ask questions, retreat, flee, oppose, or debate either. Just like me, he was assigned to a unit. He trained, he defended, he occupied, he attacked, he fired a well-aimed shot at the enemy. That's exactly what he did to me. When he hit me, he lowered his binoculars a bit and smiled, gazing at my forehead and what felt like bird droppings behind me, sprayed in the wind. He smiled when he saw he was right on the mark. When he realised he'd planted his bullet smack dab in my forehead. *Son of a bitch*, I said, when I realised he'd stuck it right in the centre.

I was impressed with him, with how skilled he was. Not an idiot like the Iranian soldier who'd hit my ear instead and ripped it clean off. The American was well-trained. He was black, but a skilled sniper. A sniper who'd probably graduated from the top military academy in America.

★

Even though the state news didn't talk about the war in the early days, we knew the Americans were coming. We were ready for a battle we didn't understand. We didn't have the guts to wonder or talk about it. They didn't tell us anything. But everyone knew they were coming: me, the officers, sergeants, platoon intelligence, grenadiers, artillery battery drivers, all the soldiers in the corps, the unit baker. Even though it was something we couldn't say on the news or make public. We didn't openly discuss it, but we whispered and found ways to talk about it covertly; we'd say something vague that each man could interpret however he liked.

In those days, the only thing we could really talk about was orders: military commanders' orders, unit orders, party celebrations and the leader's birthday! We talked about our military capability, and how we could defeat every imperialist platoon, even if their weapons were top notch and ours just pieces of junk.

The man responsible for propaganda was an officer from the countryside who barely knew how to put his trousers on straight. 'We can defeat the biggest army in the world, just by believing in our homeland and our leader,' he told us.

For this guy, whose trousers were so puffy they looked like a parachute, it meant that we, with our junk for weapons, junk for planes, junk for tanks, junk for rifles, junk for guns, that *we* could beat the biggest army in the world.

'See, we want you all to talk,' said the party official who coordinated Iraqi propaganda and combated Western propaganda.

And as the fleets advanced across the oceans, it was our job to look the other way, to refrain from acknowledging that what was there was there. After all, we were disciplined soldiers: the leader's soldiers, Republican Guard soldiers, heroes, defenders of the nation.

We didn't want to end up like Sayeed, the dumb arse with the thick glasses. He worked it out himself and told us, 'The American army's coming, it's inevitable! When the whole army's on our borders, it'll all be over for sure. They're going to attack... and if not, well then why are they here? The swarms of military battleships and planes crossing through the region, do you think they're there for a picnic?'

'But we're gonna beat them, right?' the baker asked him.

The baker was unshakable and followed the propaganda officer around like a dog. He couldn't hold his tongue. He was always asking, 'What's this? What's that?'

Sayeed shook his head in frustration.

'Maybe.' But there was doubt in his answer. He added, 'Basically, our weapons are different.'

The baker, with his pockmarked face, wasn't pleased with the response. Without pressing the matter he asked, 'What do you say we get real close to them, so our tanks and armoured vehicles face off with *their* tanks and armoured vehicles, and when we come into range, we get 'em with our bullets and grenades and handguns.'

'There's no way we'll get near them,' said thick-glasses Sayeed. 'American tank shells have a longer range than Iraqi tank shells, and that means they'll pick us off before we get near them.'

Thick-glasses Sayeed was an idiot, there's no doubt about that. But he didn't say they would pick us off like flies. He didn't say they'd scatter us across the ground like dog shit. Not at all.

'But we're gonna beat them, right?' The baker asked.

Sayeed shook his head wryly. He shook his head and slunk back to the platoon break room.

The baker wasn't happy with any of this. He informed the party propaganda officer about Sayeed. He didn't do it that morning, but by night time he'd gone into the officer's cabin and told him what happened with Sayeed, the thick idiot with the thick glasses.

The party propaganda officer didn't like men with glasses, and it wasn't just him: most platoon officers felt that way. Men with thick glasses were cowards: they didn't like war, they didn't have their hearts in it, and they weren't ready to lay down their lives, said the baker to the platoon driver.

A few days later, they hung thick-glasses Sayeed up on the wall across from the bunk hall, and then they shot him. Tata, tata, tata. Tshck tshck tshck. His glasses flew up into the air, and then hit the ground, flecked with blood. They shot him full of holes because he'd been spreading counter-propaganda to demoralise the soldiers.

The baker was one of the riflemen. He wiped his mouth with a rag. Stood towards the left of the execution squad. Blew his nose and took good aim. He brought Sayeed with the glasses to the ground like a rag riddled with bullet holes.

*

I wasn't hiding anything from them. Not one of us thought we would beat the Americans, or that we'd even win a battle. Not even the party propaganda officer himself. But we were forbidden from saying it, even the half of it. We were forbidden from thinking about it, too. So that's what happened in the first days of the war, even when the Americans started mobilising their platoons and warships, and closed in on our borders. We looked into each others' eyes like complete idiots. We were supposed to pretend we didn't know what was going on around us. We were supposed to be silent. Feign ignorance, stupidity, indifference. Even though just one look around exposed everything we couldn't say as a farce. No one had the guts to say a single word, even in jest. Exchanging that kind of news – the kind that everyone knew, but that no one spoke about– was enough to bring you down to the ground like a rag flecked with blood too, it was enough to make your brains explode in the air like bird shit in the wind.

But then suddenly everything changed. We received orders, bit by bit. They didn't say it straight out at first, but they started to be more realistic. It was clear we were preparing for war. We prepared around the clock, and soon it was time to mobilize. In the beginning we'd talked about war as a possibility, or the war 'at our gates.' Then we started talking about certain war, decisive war. It would have been stupid to think that all those preparations were just a drill, or for just the officer's fun, or because the general in command got a kick out of it.

Little by little, we started talking about the war at hand, war but not all-out war. A decisive war, no doubt. A war we needed to prepare for, a war we needed to win. Then the officers started insisting: there will be war. And we'd repeat after them: 'Yes, there will be war.'

Even the party propaganda officer, who'd denied it all from the beginning, started saying, 'Yes, there will be war.' Despite hundreds of people having been killed for saying as much just a couple days earlier! But we weren't just saying: *Yes, there will be war.* We had to follow that with another, obligatory sentence: *We're going to win, by God we're going to beat them!*

The second sentence had to answer for the first sentence's sins, or at least lighten the burden of such heavy words. And there were other things we knew in our hearts. No one could say anything about our ancient weapons that looked like they belonged to a bunch of bandits. About our faces, which looked like those of primates. About our morale, which was as low as a dog whose owner just died. Or about the men coming for us with their high tech tanks and warships and aircraft carriers to defeat us. No, not once. The propaganda officer with his parachute trousers, with his country face that looked like a piece of dough that had fallen in the oven, he believed that if we just puffed out our chests we could make their bullets tremble and fall mid-air. That our black moustaches alone, if twisted well, were enough to scatter their high-tech jets like dust in a storm.

★

The Americans will come, and they'll bring democracy. Baghdad will be like New York, Amarah will be like Chicago, Sadr City will be like Las Vegas. Ramadi will be the city of dreams, our dusty folk clothes will be no more, and our sombre faces will be replaced with clean ones, brimming with health. That's what I hoped for with all my heart, that's what I hoped for, silently, without saying a word to anyone. Without a single word that might hint at it, not to a soul on Earth, not even people I was closest to. Even that idiot baker started to have doubts. He asked me about it once when we were waiting in the truck yard to get our shiny, new bayonets. (The officers were as stupid as mules, no doubt about that. They thought we could face the Americans in battle with light artillery alone, so naturally we'd need bayonets.)

'Hey Corporal, d'you think the Americans will beat us?' he whispered nastily in my ear.

He had no more brains than a dead buffalo. He thought I was an idiot like Sayeed. He thought I was stupid enough to say *yes*, and then he'd stand in line and take aim at me with his rifle, blow his nose and then blow me to the ground like a rag to wipe the floor.

'No!' I told him.

But in my heart, I said *Yes*! And I know how to get revenge, you son of a bitch. I'll make you lick a lamb's arse for two days and then drink camel piss, you pig.

★

I said I wouldn't hide anything from any of you. I'm telling the truth today just like I did a hundred years ago. I say it without batting an eye, without a crisis of conscience. There's not much left of my honour, what with the number of insults I've had to swallow in my life, speaking to cocky men in the army, and serving fools who didn't come up to my knee. I engaged in frivolous wars that blew half my body away. That was enough to convince me that my country's problem wasn't occupation: it was that it hadn't been occupied long enough.

Right from the start, I believed we were better off with them than without them. We were talking about America, guys. Oh who do you suppose is more advanced, Baghdad or New York? Sadr City or Las Vegas? Kut or Chicago? Amarah or California, Ramadi or Miami? Oh come on, you'd be an idiot, a right idiot if you thought we were better off without America.

I wasn't the only one saying it, lots of Iraqis believed we'd be better off with them. Everything they'd bring us would be wrapped in cellophane. Everything would be new, still in its box, and wrapped in cellophane. It'd be like flowers on your birthday. Everything they'd bring us would be delightful, they'd bring us happiness itself. American soldiers weren't angels, sure, but it wasn't their job to be. I firmly believed that if they said they'd do something, they would. I believed them. I was as sure of this as I was sure of myself, my salary, my ear that fell into my pocket, my shattered ribs, and my stomach ruined by gunpowder, hunger, and beatings.

I'm telling you, I didn't have the slightest doubt about any of it. The Americans would bring everything great to our crummy country. They'd come to our streets choked with dust and flies, and everything they'd bring would be brilliant white like a young girl's tits. The Americans would give me back the ear that fell into my pocket. They'd fix my ribs and intestines, they'd remove the shrapnel still lodged in my body, and they'd tell me, 'You're just great, Mister Sobhan.'

I just love the idea of the word 'mister' leaving their lips. I'm not kidding, I swear. 'Mister' is the greatest word any man on Earth can say. You think I'm making too big a deal? Guys, these are Americans, after all, not Saddam's party members. And whoever doubted it was the biggest idiot on the face of the earth.

★

I prepared myself well for war. Instead of cleaning my gun, oiling my rifle, and counting bullets for battle, instead of squad attention, stand at ease, squad turn to the right in file, and other futile preparations, I was readying what I needed to welcome them. I put flowers in my pocket, and learned a few English words so we could understand each other. I was practically delirious with joy. I stood next to the other soldiers and felt like I was grinning to myself, just remembering that they'd be here in just a few days. I felt like my heart was jumping for joy, that it might fly out of my chest like a bird. That's what egged the baker on and kindled his doubt. Even the party propaganda officer with the parachute trousers started monitoring me.

'Why are you so happy?' The baker asked me once.

'I'm happy… because we're going to win!' I said. And then he shut up.

The war didn't last long. It was a walk in the park. The first shot sent my ears ringing. It sent a voice into the ear drum of my missing ear, a voice saying that the time for change had come. The key was turning in the door. The moment had come for things to change. And on that day in particular I felt like there was another side to things, that a rainstorm was coming to wash everything clean. To wash away the dust that had stifled our lungs.

'The American army is advancing.'

The wind howled so loud, like a woman wailing.

Early the next morning, the propaganda officer sent a

squadron of soldiers to get a sense of what the enemy meant to do. But the soldiers made a blunder out of their mission. They dragged their huge leather shoes through the heavy mud as the storm pushed them on, to the beat of a military march, to the beat of the propaganda officer's voice. They came back two days later all out of step. I felt like they'd been defeated without ever fighting a battle.

'We'll be here, on this hill,' the officer said.

Near the hill was a fish market, and rubbish piles littered with dead cats, and all day the wind blew the foul stench our way.

'Couldn't we have picked someplace better?' I thought to myself.

'It's a strategic position!' The officer with the parachute trousers said.

But no one passed by our strategic position. The American forces went straight to Baghdad and brought down the statue of the president. The baker and the party propaganda officer vanished that day, and no one heard from them again. They disappeared into the storm like shadows. The ground we stood on began to smell like corpses. Food disappeared from the squadron shop. The baker, the driver, and the dogs were all gone. The only dog left was the commander's. It used to eat from the squadron's garbage, now it went out looking for something to eat and found nothing.

'You should take the idea of "winning the war" with a grain of salt. You really need to take a historical perspective on it all. America's better, even for the dogs,' a teacher who'd been drafted told the officers, trying to convince them to surrender.

★

There we were, waiting for the Americans. I washed my face twice that morning, and got the flower in my pocket ready. I climbed the hill.

'Halt!' They shouted.

'Friends...' I answered, in English.

And before my hand reached my pocket, I heard the shot.

The silent sun trickled through a cloud of dust. Something like shattered glass was dripping from my head. Deserts of rubble fell from me. I imagined I heard the blood's soft voice as it flowed from my body, somewhere. The black American turned towards me, smiling. Looked carefully at his shot. The only noise that reached him was the noise coming from my head.

'Son of a bitch!'

It must've been a figment of my imagination. For some strange reason, I didn't believe that I was dead. I felt something else, something closer to terror, a tangled mess of fears I couldn't even explain to myself.

*

I ascended to the heavens. As soon as I could see, I spotted TV antennas. Soldiers' berets flying up like a murder of crows at first dawn. Worn underclothes. Discarded plastic bags. Rubbish rising up from Iraq. I felt, for the first time, an end to worry and sighs, I felt like my soul had slipped through a hole in the sky and fallen through itself, then entered an endless corridor, and I started gasping. At the end of the corridor stood an angel.

'Who are you?' He asked.

'Corporal Sobhan.'

'Who?'

'Corporal Sobhan... don't you know who I am? I'm the one whose brains got splattered by an American sniper, just like bird shit. I'm a war hero, a martyr, and Saddam Hussein said martyrs go straight to heaven: they get a free pass, and get in right away.'

Skepticism began to cloud the angel's face.

'But you reached into your pocket to present the sniper with a flower, didn't you?' He asked with raised eyebrows and a gesture.

'Yes, I did. Is that what's keeping a decision from being made?'

'Of course,' said the angel. 'You wanted to give your enemy a flower, and now you want to be considered a martyr? You can't truly be serious.'

I stared into the angel's face like an idiot, wishing he would give me a straight answer.

'O kind angel, what do you make of me: martyr or not?'

'That depends. You're not a martyr, but you're not a regular casualty, either. At this point, you'll need to wait with the other unresolved cases.'

His response cheered me up a bit. It gave me a bit of hope; maybe in the end

I'd get lucky, become a martyr, and get into heaven. I thought about this for a minute.

'This has happened to me all my life, O dear angel,' I told him. 'I was stuck in limbo for a long time when I was promoted to corporal, because the officers found out I'd taken two days more vacation than I was allowed, and so it took longer for them to recognise my new rank. Inside the unit I was a corporal. But... a corporal in limbo. See, I've often been in limbo: a corporal in limbo, a martyr in limbo... can I ask you, O dear angel, will I have to stay like this for long?'

'In truth, time is immeasurable here. We are in eternity here, as you know. Your journey to the end of this corridor has taken a hundred years.'

'Are you serious? My journey took a hundred years... that's amazing. Could I see what happened to my country in all that time?'

'Just concern yourself with yourself. Don't trouble yourself with the matters of people on earth. Besides, there are many others like you here. We haven't finished the Ancient

Greek period yet; in other words, you've got a long wait ahead.'

'So where should I go?'

'You could take a stroll around. You're allowed in this area.'

'Thank you, O kind angel,' I said, and turned a bit to face the great throne on which God was sitting. A short man was facing him, speaking confidently. I turned back to the angel.

'O angel... O angel! Just one last question – who's that man that God is judging, isn't that some American actor? I think I've seen him before, in a Hollywood film they show on Channel 7 in Iraq.'

'Him? Of course not... didn't I tell you we're still working on the Ancient Greek period? That's Socrates, of whom you've heard. The philosopher, Socrates.'

Socrates, with his bald, dome-like head, was arguing with God, asking question after question.

'Socrates, you are asking quite a lot of questions,' said God, growing angry. 'You must answer what I am asking you.'

'Yes my Lord, you are right. But I believe that sending so many prophets to the people of earth confuses them; they find it all beyond belief. Instead, it would be far better if you released one of the dead, from time to time, to leave his grave and tell people what happened to him.'

It was clear that God found some sense in what Socrates was saying. He fell silent and stroked his chin, thinking.

Why not take advantage of this opportunity and ask him to send me down to earth? I thought to myself. I raised my hand, and as soon as the Lord noticed, he shouted, 'Who are you?'

'Corporal Sobhan, my Lord.'

'Who?'

'Corporal Sobhan, my Lord, I'm the one whose brains the American sniper splattered, like bird droppings into the wind. I thought I was a martyr, but it sounds like my case is still under consideration. Seeing as the matter is going to take a while, why not order me to be sent down to earth, my Lord? As a dead man who awoke from his grave, to tell the people of earth what I've seen. You know I come from a region that's caused problems in the world… and I want to see what's happened to my country after the war.'

God paused for a moment, and then nodded. Socrates smiled, and the angel got ready to carry me down to the people of the earth.

*

Dear gentlemen, I am telling you the truth: as I descended to Kut, I felt that a change had occurred during my journey. It all felt very different from my ascent to the heavens. I'd seen rubbish flying up from Kut in all directions during my ascent: gunpowder, plastic bags, tattered underclothes, auto parts from the junkyard, crows, flies…. My descent was completely different.

'I think you might've made a mistake,' I told the angel when he placed me on a cloud for a break.

'Made a mistake? Have you gone mad?' The angel chastised me.

He carried me from the cloud where he'd put me, holding me by my shirt collar while I kicked as if I was swimming in space, and I flew. Oh, what ecstasy, what bliss, as I flew through the air. Suddenly a shape materialised, appearing before my eyes – it was Kut, like a pair of soft, parted lips, her golden day waking with the light. Her river recumbent, reclining. It looked like heaven, her lights not veiled by dust, her bold breasts like a deluge of moons. As we got closer, I saw paradise-like changes. Light reached the heavens on the wind, water mixed with earth. I smiled as the angel and I approached through wispy white clouds surrounding the city. Bit by bit, I saw it was Kut. The river was the first thing I recognised; the Tigris of course, its bends like a wriggling snake, green earth around its banks. Its light, pure waters, translucent blue in the depths. Towering trees around the grassy ground.

'Is this Las Vegas? Manhattan? Miami? What happened to my city, choked with flies and dust like somewhere in Pakistan? How was it transformed into such a magnificent city? I cried and laughed, and asked the angel, 'O angel of the Lord, tell me honestly, have we come to the wrong place? Did you get dizzy? Did you get turned around, and head north instead of south? It happens! Drivers in Iraq do it! You tell him you're going to the city of Kut, he takes you to somewhere else! He says he's lost and steals your money too! Are you lost, mate… could be! I won't tell God. I won't tell on you, I wouldn't want him to punish you. Just tell me what city you've taken me to.'

'Kut,' said the Lord's angel, without another word.

'The Kut I knew was more like a Pakistani village!' I told him. 'You couldn't walk two feet without your nose filling with dust from the road, without sweating like you'd stuck your head in the oven, without the flies swarming at your eyes like they were two pools of spit.'

The Lord's angel wouldn't keep carrying me while I argued with him like that. He told me to be quiet: he was an angel of the Lord after all, the real deal, no imitation. An angel of the heavens, not a plastic one made in China. In my day, China manufactured pictures of our imams, embroidered prayers, religious banners, prayer beads, incense burners, and so on. This, on the other hand, was an angel, straight from the source! I brought him from the heavens, an angel crafted by God, no forgery manufactured in a Saudi or Iranian factory.

So could he have gotten it wrong? He couldn't have. I figured I'd be quiet and see where this ended up.

'O angel of the Lord, let me down where I lost my life, where my head was blown off by the American sniper. There, right near the river, on the hill we used as a military position in the war, by the rotting fish market and the rubbish where they throw the dead cats.'

The angel made a big arc, cutting a wide circle in the air, and with a single graceful movement he landed gently. He stopped. He carefully set me down on my feet, somewhere spacious and clean, near the gate of a big building, made of clear glass. The building was so tall I couldn't count how many floors there were, maybe a hundred. It looked like a skyscraper, with a tower piercing the sky. The bright sun was reflected in the glass, and a couple of women were walking through the entrance. The ground was paved with smooth white stones. The street across the way was fairly wide, surrounded by big trees on either side shading the pavement, and a cool, sweet breeze blew from their shadow. It eased the heat of the midmorning sun.

'This is where you were killed,' the angel of the Lord said. He turned towards the sky, and in a moment he had disappeared.

I landed gently. I felt my face with my hands. I looked around.

The thing that struck me was the metro gate across from the big building, the metro that Iraqis had awaited for so long. Across the glass threshold there was a big sign, written in transliterated Arabic: *Bawabet Al-Hubb* – Gate of Love.

God, I said, have they changed the names too? A nearby street sign read *Al-Ushaq Avenue* – Lover's Avenue, and a big park with a wall nearly six feet high was called *Jana'n Al-Rahmeh* – Gardens of Compassion.

*

Gentlemen, I spent three hours strolling down the big avenue across from the Metro of Love, through the Gardens of Compassion, *Zuqaq Al-Tasamuh* – Goodwill Lane, *Maktabet Al-Shuara' Al-Suada'* – Happy Poets Library, *Mat'am Al-Tabi'ato Al-Jamileh* – Nature's Splendour Restaurant. People passed in front of me, smiling. They were dressed in smart, clean clothes, like they were going to a party. Their faces shone with good health. Their bodies were athletic, like Spartan youth. In that moment, I recognised the square that used to be filled with beggars, and I stopped right before it. There were columns of radiant glass, and a big sign with the name: *Sahat Al-Amal* – Hope Square. It was beautiful now, with lots of fountains shooting right out of the ground in time with music. A bunch of children were playing happily near the tall trees. Sure, I knew it was Kut Square. The square where they had once executed deserters. About five minutes later I stood in front of the hill where my head was shot off. Behind it was a building. They had preserved the front, and named it *Tallat Al-Musiqa* – Music Hill. A band was playing peaceful songs, and in front of them, several lovers were dancing.

*

At Friendship Corner, I stopped a handsome man with his arm around a dark young woman's shoulder. The man was in his thirties, very smartly dressed, and his smile was the first thing I noticed.

'Hey mate, I've got a question,' I called out to him.

He was startled at first, and then stopped. He looked at me, and the expression on his face changed.

'Pardon?' He said in soft, dulcet Arabic.

'Yes, I have a question: is this the city of Kut?'

'Indeed, that it is. But why are you speaking so angrily, has something injured you? Is there something the matter?'

'Me? No, not at all, I'm not angry. I just think your voice is really low; you're speaking in a different language to the one I left the people of Kut speaking a hundred years ago.'

'A hundred years ago?' He replied, confused.

'Yeah. I'm an Iraqi soldier who was killed here in the city of Kut during the war with the Americans a hundred years ago.'

I felt like the man didn't believe me, as if he'd stumbled across one of the People of the Cave. (That's a story from the

Quran, about a group of people who believed in Christianity during the time of an unjust ruler who was persecuting them. To protect them, God froze them for a hundred years, and when they came back, they discovered that the city had become Christian, and everybody there knew their story.)

It was clear from the way he spoke that the man was surprised. I was talking in highly explosive capital letters that sounded like battle. Whereas today, the people of the city spoke so serenely. Their voices came out softly, tenderly.

'Democracy must have even changed your voices!' I said, and thought to myself, *America – didn't I tell you America could work miracles?*

'To be honest, I don't understand what you are saying. Forgive me please, and calmly tell me what you want, so I can help you.'

Meanwhile, the young woman at his side soothed me with a sweet smile and a heartfelt laugh.

'Listen, sir, I'm an Iraqi soldier who was killed a hundred years ago, my story's a long one, I don't know if you've heard the tale of Corporal Sobhan or not! Just like the Christians of old heard the tale of the People of the Cave!'

'Forgive me, I'm not familiar with it.'

'Basically, I'm Corporal Sobhan, whose brains an American sniper splattered like bird shit, right here on top of this hill! I went straight up to the heavens. But the day of judgement is taking a long time; there's lots of wars – Iraq's wars and the Muslim's wars, and they take time, there's lots of casualties and martyrs; the battles of the market in Kut from back then need ages for God to divide the good from the bad and judge them. Our problem, don't you know what our problem is? You see, the age of the prophets is over: a wise Greek man suggested that from time to time, God send one of the dead to preach and spread religion. And so God picked me, he picked Corporal Sobhan, he told me. see here Corporal Sobhan, go to Kut and preach to the people. So in short: I came back to the city I was killed in, the city of Kut, to spread religion. I'm not a prophet, but I've been sent to preach.'

'Religion? We have no need for religion, sir! Learning about God's justice and laws is for barbarians! The problem is that people interpret religion however they see fit, to support their own barbarism and savagery. We have no need for that, we are civilised folk. We know God, we govern by God's justice, love, forgiveness, and equality between all people. Whoever has God has no need for religion.'

'What do you mean you don't need religion?'

'We've no need for it at all; why should we? We've managed without it for quite a long time, and things are much better than they were before. We learnt that the blissfulness of religious existence makes people cruel-hearted, just as any kind of faith does. It desensitises them.'

'I can barely believe this. How does life go on when people live without religion?'

'Quite the opposite, in fact – it's been years since this city has seen a single dispute. There are no more Sunnis, Shi'as, Christians, or Jews. No more conflicts or civil wars, and no one judges anyone else over his religion.'

'Really? There's something I want to know, but please don't make fun of me… are you sure that I'm in Kut? Or did I end up in some other city?'

'Yes, you are in Kut. Sir, you are here in the civilised world, where we have no need for religion. Many wars have been sparked by extremism, religion, sectarianism, and so on. But thank God, who delivered us from religion. We've grown so happy without it. He who has God has no need for religion.'

'You're right, but there's something else I want to know. Has all this happened thanks to democracy, or….'

'I'm not sure how it happened, exactly. But history has taken a big turn. Just take America: now it's an extremist state, gripped by religion.'

'America became an extremist state?'

'Yes, you didn't know that? It looks like you really don't know where you are, sir.'

'Right. Like I told you, I was killed a hundred years ago during the war, when the Americans came and occupied Iraq, for democracy's sake.'

'Ah, well. We know history quite well. The problem, as you recall, was that sectarian war broke out right after American democracy. People hated the way things were; they hated bigotry, hatred, and terrorism, and started to hunt down extremists. The extremists found refuge in America, and that's the problem now. America has become an extremist state, overrun by religious intolerance. Religious radicals destroyed their buildings and civilisation... it's become like Afghanistan was a hundred years ago, when it was ruled by the Taliban.'

'Are you telling the truth, sir?'

'Yes, of course. Do you doubt me?'

'To be honest, I... how could I have doubts. I've been dead for a hundred years. But I feel like an idiot. What you're saying is hard to believe. Has America given up on democracy?'

'Yes, America is a rogue state now. It's part of the axis of evil. The civilised world is trying to bring the country back to its senses and bring back democracy...'

'Good Lord, what are you saying? Who is part of the civilised world, sir?'

'The three civilised, industrialised, democratic nations: Iraq, Saudi Arabia, and Iran! As you know, after Iraq's transition to democracy, the religious governments in the other two nations fell, and they became secular, democratic countries.'

'Iran and Saudi Arabia?'

'Yes, they are now the vanguard of the civilised world, just like Iraq. The problem is with the West – that's right, the problem is with the West, which has been transformed into an oasis of terrorism, a haven for religious intolerance and hatred. We have a great duty, sir, to restore democracy to these countries and make the world a safer place. But please excuse me, I'm pressed for time; my girlfriend and I want to go to this event and donate a few things to American refugee children. If you're looking for a place to relax, there's a wonderful artsy coffee shop at the end of this street. You could have a bite to eat, or some tea or coffee. It's all free, for people who don't have any money on them.'

'Thanks for telling me. Goodbye, sir, goodbye sir, God bless. Helping take care of our brothers, the Americans and the Europeans, their refugees. They deserve to be taken care of, after their countries' dictatorships.'

I slapped my forehead. What was going on! Really, was the world still spinning the right way? What has this man said, about Iraq saving the American people from dictatorship, and bringing them back their freedom... and then the whole thing about American refugees in Iraq, could that be right? Iraq offering refugee status, freedom of expression, and other things to Americans who were persecuted in their own country? Did that angel get me drunk before he brought me back to earth? Honestly, I don't know whether to go to the coffee shop or find out whether all this is true.

I walked about a hundred yards and stopped in front of the wonderful artsy coffee shop.

There was a television out front, and I drank some orange juice, served to me by a pretty waitress. She brought it out on a platter embossed with silver, and set it in front of me on the table.

'Ma'am, could I ask you a question?'

'Of course, go right ahead.'

'Are you from Kut?'

'No sir, I'm from Nasiriyah, I just work here.'

'Nasiriyah? Ah, Nasiriyah. I remember Nasiriyah; I was born in Nasiriyah. Has it developed too, has it become like Kut?'

'Oh even more so, sir. But I just work here – my husband is from Kut, and I'm from Nasiriyah, the Flower of the South, the most advanced city of all.'

'God, I can hardly believe it...'

'Would you like anything else?'

The newscast had begun, and the president of Iraq appeared on the television screen with his dog in front of a big building.

'Is that the president of Iraq?' I asked her.

'Yes, standing in front of the Green House, and that's his dog. He's going to give an important speech about the war against religious extremism in America, human rights violations, and of course violations of women's rights and freedom of expression...'

'Ah, well then I'll listen to what he has to say.'

★

Believe me, gentlemen, that's everything that happened! While I was watching the news on television two men walked in and came towards me. They looked like police, I could tell by their clothes and the insignia they wore. They stood right in front of me, and I looked up at them.

'Sir, may we kindly see your papers?' The skinnier, younger one said.

'To be honest, I haven't got any papers....'

'You're under suspicion – you're an American, sir, you have the air of someone angry, and religious; there's a note of terrorism in your booming, explosive voice.'

'No sir, not at all,' I begged. 'That kind of talk is passé, from an earlier era in this country... back then, it was fine to talk like this, it wasn't terrorism.'

'Are you Iraqi?'

'Yes, I swear. I'm Corporal Sobhan, haven't you studied history? Don't any of you write about me? I'm the one whose brains were splattered like bird shit by an American sniper. I'm a war hero, a martyr, if you still don't recognise me, I swear, my case is still under review, I came here to spread religion –'

'Religion?'

'Yes, religion.'

'So you admit you're a terrorist?'

'Listen, I swear, it's not like that at all, let me tell you. Listen to me, wait a minute, just hold on, before I go with you...'

★

The rain began to fall that afternoon, lightly at first, and then harder, striking tall glass buildings and showering the trees. The rain lasted for about twenty-five minutes, and then it left patches of blue sky behind. After the clouds receded, cascades of light descended. White steam began to rise up from the tarmac on the long street, and cars gleamed as they drove by. There were boats with white sails in the Tigris, and above Kut were delicate clouds. Reedy music poured down from the balconies.

A lawyer mentioned that the *Kut Observer* had omitted two facts: first, that her client faced terrorism charges, and second, that the newspaper failed to cover an important piece of news from America, news of rumours sweeping the nation that the Antichrist had appeared in Iraq.

The Worker

Diaa Jubaili

Translated by Andrew Leber

To the Head of the *Governing Council of Basra*
Office of the Governor General
Memo: Consultation

Regarding Your Excellency's enquiry as to the possible existence of historical occurrences more horrendous, more extensive, or at least equal to the unfortunate phenomena and bloody events of the past few years. You requested our counsel – for which we are grateful – in finding examples that match or surpass the tragedies and catastrophes which have occurred in our dear city since the disastrous exhaustion of our oil and gas, which are as follows (pursuant to the list that you provided us within your correspondence):

1. Mass killings via explosions or demolition of residential buildings, including those committed by terrorist groups
2. Famine, leading to such measures as the consumption of stray cats and dogs by hungry residents
3. Sale of, and trade in, children and young women
4. Homelessness and extreme poverty
5. Spread of sickness and epidemics, especially the plague
6. Ethnic purges
7. Widespread theft and looting
8. Unemployment

In accordance with your desires, we group of experts in the field of history, appointed at the behest of Your Excellency as advisors, have conducted research deep within various volumes and the oldest archives of humanity. We return with a summary that we here enclose. May you find it helpful to peruse, that our service to your Excellency may reflect upon us as though a gleaming crown, as we give honour to your exalted personage.

Note: Regarding Your Lordship's counsel on the statues in the city, we think it unwise to maintain them without sparing a thought for exploiting the material they are made of - bronze. We therefore present our recommendation that these statues be removed for sale, so that their value may be employed in the public interest.

*

The Governor set aside the memo and began to sift through the papers beneath it. He was the latest in a long line of religious strongmen who had taken power in the city since the British-American occupation, a century before. Clearly he approved of the recommendations made by the Council of Advisors, the fruit of their research piled up in the yellow file opened in front of him on the heavy wooden table. You could see it in the slight smile that flickered across his lips – with maybe a hint of craftiness – before disappearing beneath his other twitches. Then, he pulled a set of prayer beads – black with an amber gloss – from his jacket pocket, and began muttering words, as if reciting a prayer, like the one-hundred-and-one glorifications, perhaps, one for each of the beads.

He stopped every three or four beads – the muttering increasing, his lips rippling like he was trying to dislodge something stuck in his mouth from breakfast.

When it came time for the Governor's monthly address, he would commit the first hour of the day to these spiritual exercises. Instead of the usual stack of papers – agreements and protocols and decrees for signing, carried in by an aide at the start of the day – he would sit with the historians' compilations and refresh his memory on historical events more violent and chaotic than the city's current afflictions.

Once he got underway, the Governor would slowly relax, sinking back into his luxurious chair. He would close his eyes or raise his head a little, his thumbs and fingers never stopping as they worked through the prayer beads. His jacket sleeve would lift up from time to time, revealing a thick silver watch that illuminated its surroundings with its digital screen. Then he would start clicking through the web, often to check out a YouTube clip from his latest sermon.

Once satisfied with what he planned to say, he would prepare himself to appear on the large television screen in Umm al-Burum Square[1], to give his infamous sermons to the people.

He would adjust his attire in front of a gold-framed mirror, checking to make sure there were no stray hairs or missed buttons. Then he would sit facing the camera set up by his desk. Behind him, a picture of himself gesturing to the gathered crowds from within a white, heavily armored maglev car, his hand heavy with bejeweled rings of agate, ruby, turquoise. Blond, bulky American bodyguards surrounded the car, laden with deadly weaponry.

The Governor would often invite a group of journalists to his study whenever an enormous explosion, an atrocious massacre, or some other crisis stormed through the city and left thousands of dead, crippled, and demented in its wake. He would charm them for hours, his cultured words unfolding as though composed for a rhetoric competition on some religious program. All of these flatterers would gape at him just like the simple villagers in Umm al-Burum square. They were in awe of the Governor's logic, his deftness with words, his skill for devising the cleverest phrases.

On that particular day, the Governor sat in his usual place, cleared his throat with a few bismallahs, and a few prayers, then recited the names of God and cursed the devils in the room, as well as all critics and unbelievers. Then he began his sermon of justification:

'You know, dear brothers and sisters, that we live in the shadow of a dire crisis, much as we pray with all our hearts and souls that this affliction be lifted from our nation. Yet this does not mean that the crisis is unprecedented in the history of nations past and present. All who think otherwise are certainly mistaken. My brothers and sisters, let me reassure you that my government is sparing no effort and utilizing all power at its disposal to discover new sources of energy to compensate for our sharp loss of wealth.

'As you know, in not-so-distant times people relied on coal to make their lives easier. Perhaps the thought occurred to one of them: "What if the coal runs out one day?" But look at what happened next – it was not too long before they discovered oil! Yes, and when our oil and gas ran out we came across uranium. When the uranium was used up we searched and searched until we found mercury. No sooner had the mercury run out than we started looking for other sources of wealth, like solar power or the precious bronze that sprawled out before us in our gardens and public squares, in the form of these useless, trivial figures.

'It is true that utterly disgraceful things have happened; acts reminiscent of infidel tyrants, murderous sultans. Yet all of these events are nothing compared to what happened before, in terms of the extent of destruction and the depth of the tragedy involved. So let me say…

'It is not astonishing that a building or two is blown up after being worn away by time and wear. Let us compare, for example, with New York more than one hundred years ago, when terrorists attacked the two towers of the World Trade Center. The airplanes turned them to ruins!

'It is irrational for us to be shocked that the city is subjected to similar events right now. These tragedies have caused the deaths of thousands, yes, but many more thousands, millions indeed, starve to death in the forests of Africa or the mud of India. Here are just some examples of ruinous famines that have made a mockery of humanity with the losses they caused'.

The Governor picked up a thick packet of papers from the table beside him and began to leaf through them on camera.

'Ibn Khaldun[2] relates that the people of Talmisan – in the year 1304 – were forced to eat corpses, cats, and rats. You might think that was just a rumour Ibn Khaldun spread about, but the matter was put to rest, I would argue, by Ibn al-Ahmar[3], who confirmed that the residents of Talmisan did indeed dine on each other. On top of this, they would empty out their own bowels and dry the contents in the sun, before cooking it up and feeding it to their children!

'And don't let me start on the lesser cities of ancient Egypt where people on the Upper Nile ate their children, or Timbuktu where half the residents of died of hunger. Let us think of Iraq specifically, taking the famine of 1918 as an example.'

He flipped ahead several pages.

'The Iraqi researcher Abd al-Aziz al-Qassab[4] relates to us in his writings what he saw en route from Aleppo to Mosul. When he entered the village of Damir Qabu he witnessed long lines of starving people waiting for their turn to grab a piece of meat from a dead animal – I believe it was dog! Furthermore, there were those who gathered up the blood of slaughtered animals to eat later.'[5]

Here, he held up a yellowing document, the spindly script barely legible.

'I have here an old copy of a Turkish newspaper from that time, which carries a remarkable dialogue between a judge and a woman – an ugly, short criminal type. Her sallow face was apparently covered with red spots, like smallpox. She and her husband, known as Aboud, and no less ugly, conspired to kidnap children or buy them. Then they would slaughter them, cook their meat, and sell it to the people. The government found nearly a hundred little skulls in her house, in addition to a great number of other bones, piled up in a pit in her basement.

'In the end, the court found that there was no choice but to execute both of them. When the time came to carry out the execution, they were carried on the backs of two donkeys on their way to Bab al-Tuub in Mosul, where two hangman's nooses had been prepared for them. They endured their share of cursing and spitting from the crowd on their way. Aboud, the husband, hurled curses back at the crowd with arrogance in his eyes.

'Once they were hanged, the mothers of their victims came forward to tear at the criminals' feet with their teeth. One of those women screamed as she gnawed on a piece of the woman's leg, 'They ate three of my children!'

The Governor paused, looking up from his papers to look straight at the camera. 'So – what do you think, then?

'If you want, I could tell you shocking tales that happened during the great famines in China, the Soviet Union, Bangladesh, Ukraine, Ireland, Biafra, North Korea, Zimbabwe, Somalia... And that's leaving out all the famines in Europe and all the other continents during the Middle Ages – but it would take too long! The questions that occur to me now seem to be as follows:

'Have any of you eaten your children? Have any of you defecated, then dried what came out to cook it and eat it? Have any of you reached the point where you're hungry enough to steal children, cook their flesh, and sell what's left to the starving at a discount?

'I therefore advise you all to look around and not complain, since complaining is the hallmark of the hypocrite. Give thanks that you have not yet reached such a terrifying level of hunger! As for eating cats and insects and stray dogs, I feel this is a sign of shortages the world over, and not in our country specifically.

'Think upon what has befallen others – and prepare yourselves!

Here he turned to pick up a slender volume from off the table, flipping to a marked section before turning back to the camera.

'As for the matter of epidemics, I would like to pause here. I think we'll agree that nothing really has happened to our dear city if we compare it with, say, what happened in Europe during the Black Death. In my hand right now is a strange and curious tale from the time of that deadly plague, about how it began and how it spread on the old continent. A gifted Central Asian storyteller narrates a tale of his Tatar ancestor, and how one ordinary war was transformed overnight into one of putrid biological warfare. If you like, I shall read you the whole story, although in the voice of the Tatar narrator of course.

'Listen closely, then:

On the Crimean peninsula, in the time of my ancestors, there was a disastrous battle that took place between my Tatar forefathers and the Venetians, whose colonies had extended far beyond the walls of Italy. Those Venetians were fortified in an impregnable fortress, one that was far harder to storm than the Tatar commander would have liked.

The Tatar soldiers were brave however – none of them wearied or complained about the Venetian defences. That is, until the plague started to spread among them, and individuals and then whole battalions began to drop. Given how much their commander took pride in his troops, it was almost too much to see his valiant men writhing about, from the fever and the pain, like headless chickens.

The encampment seemed to fill with the excrement of the afflicted soldiers, and the corpses piled up everywhere. As the Tatar commander watched this, growing more mortified by the second, an idea occurred to him. He ordered his soldiers to load up the catapults with the rotten corpses and fire them into the Venetian fortress. Of course, the only problem with this was the ignoble position my particular antecedent found himself in, as I will relate to you.

This man lived out a miserable existence during this time as a cowardly fighter, who could not have stood up to a Venetian mouse. He hated war and sacrifice, thinking them silly ideas sadly lodged deep in most men's minds. Therefore, he thought it best to think of a way to successfully flee from that hellish place, much as he knew doing so would entail a great deal of danger – perhaps ending in death. This all makes me want to bury my head in shame – I tell it to you now for the first time since I heard it from my father, who heard it from my grandfather, who heard it from his father... and so on.

And so, on a pitch black night, when many of his comrades were meeting their fate and succumbing to the sickness, my ancestor tried to sneak out of the Tatar camp. Yet all of a sudden he found his way blocked by a wall of gleaming horsemen, charged with guarding the encampment. He stopped behind a tree and thought of what he might do in the meantime.

In the end, he found there was nothing for it but to bury himself among the corpses of the plague dead, and was carried off with four other corpses to one of the catapults and was projected high into the night sky. He twisted in the air for a few seconds, trying to keep from screaming as he thought of how he would die the moment he hit the ground, all hope of escape dashed.

My ancestor felt a rumbling in his stomach, and nearly expelled his leavings like a bird in flight, when he noticed the ruinous losses the plague had inflicted on the Tatar ranks below him. He thought for an instant of becoming a bird himself, of sprouting two wings and flying away.

You might not believe what happened next.

My forefather came to no harm. He fell on a cart filled with hay, then rolled until he came to rest alongside other Tartar corpses hurled by the catapult. There were other corpses of dead Venetians who had been struck by the attack.

The Venetians were so shocked by the sight of corpses raining down upon them that it took three whole days before they thought to begin setting fired to them. My ancestor realised that he could no longer pretend to be one of the corpses or he'd be burned alive.

So he put on the uniform of one of the dead Venetians and waited until the smell of the dead and burned corpses filled the fortress. From there it was only too easy to slink away to one of the anchored ships that was filled with fleeing people, bound for Sicily. This was at a time when the Black Death had all of Europe in its embrace.

He snapped the book shut and set it aside.

'The story is over, my brothers and sisters! Do you understand now? Can you imagine what I'm thinking about now? Questions like: Have any of you been hurled from a catapult with rotten corpses? Know that the terrible state this Tatar soldier reached is the worst thing that could happen to a person in the middle of a deadly epidemic like the Black Death in Europe.

'All we experience now are a few diseases spreading here and there, like cholera and measles, tuberculosis and leprosy, maybe even AIDS. Yet none of you has yet approached that horrendous state of affairs that existed on the Old Continent.

'There is nothing I can do on this painful occasion other than promise you, by the very beard and moustache you see before you, that things have not reached the point of firing rotting corpses into the air with catapults or even with cannons. I will take decisive action to save what can be saved, but you must know that what is happening in our dear city could easily happen in any other city. Do you understand, my beloved friends?

'As for the selling and enslavement of children, there will always be some father who sells his children out of dire hunger. Or he might need to provide a child with food and all the necessary things in life, yet find his pockets empty. Other societies experience this – even if it seems unnatural to see it in our society at present, it is a long-standing state of affairs elsewhere.

'We know that the trade in children is a serious matter, about which we cannot be silent. Yet things have not reached the point where we have open markets for slave-trading. If we cast a discerning glance over the path of prior nations, the size of our current calamity would shrink in comparison.

'Our people would then remember that Basra itself was never more than a small store where a boy or a young woman might be sold. In comparison, other cities were riotous trading floors for all manner of bodies and manpower, to be employed in all manner of physical tasks or vile sexual ends.

'So it is with other matters – unemployment, terrorism, ethnic purges, looting, poverty, homelessness and so on. All are detestable, of course, and one cannot celebrate at a time when the fallen are all around us. Yet we also must be realistic; we cannot simply wrap ourselves in victimhood without being more understanding of how these curses have afflicted other nations.

'For terrorism is widespread all over the civilized world, likewise ethnic purges. I have no wish to bring up the Armenian massacre in Turkey, nor the Holocaust of the Jews in Germany, nor other sites of slaughter in Rwanda, Yugoslavia, Palestine, Lebanon and Iraq decades ago.

'No doubt there was some looting and theft during the terrible floods and storms in America as well. In all the countries that used to look down upon our people and call for us to be 'civilized,' all it takes is one fire to ignite, one volcano to erupt, one earthquake to rumble and all the looters and robbers you can image will pour forth from all directions.

'Even with unemployment, there are some advanced nations that, only yesterday, were great capitalist empires, but today have become effectively socialist states. But don't bother asking them, 'Where are the jobs for the rest of the world?' So instead of demonstrating, my dear friends, instead of squawking out those protest slogans to no end – all of which only benefit foreigners, naturally – let us stand together in solidarity. We can identify points of weakness and negativity, then plan to root them out of our beloved lands.

'By way of example, and as a question for you all, tell me: what use is the presence of these dumb idols that stare off into nothingness? They stand everywhere, at the crossroads and the public squares. Do we need them, living as we do in a place that hates idols? We already know that these useless statues were the work of hacks and hypocrites, second-rate artists at best. Now they serve as little more than meeting points for drug runners and addicts!

'Therefore, my brothers and sisters, I have seen fit to order these ruined idols turned into fuel to light the future, beginning from tomorrow.

★

In Umm al-Burum square, the pops and hisses of static started to overpower the Governor's voice as he gazed down on the masses of people from an enormous screen.

'... in me, my beloved friends, my dear brothers and sisters. Look at what has befallen others and believe me, my friends, that what has befallen you is not as bad as the feeling of poison coursing through your veins. I promise you... I will look into... kssssssshhhhhh... I hope to ta... kssssshhhh... ay that all poss... and end to all terri... here at your service, from you... ksshh... kssshhh... kssssssssshhhhhhhhh-'

The broadcast was cut off, the screen going dark.

A cry went up from the gathered mobs. Curses and spitting could be heard, grumbling along with the rumbling of empty stomachs. Before long the people dispersed, each taking their way home, until the square was deserted – aside from a few corpses strewn here and there, of course.

All, that is, except for one man carrying a hammer, dressed in overalls. All, that is, except for me.

I jumped from the concrete plinths where I had stood just moments before, leaving behind my enormous hammer. As the others departed – no handout today, it seemed – none turned to watch me grab hold of the corpses and drag them over to a waiting cart.

In 2103, just as the last of the city's oil and gas had run out, the last automaton also stopped working. It was hurled into the open grave of automatons in the dried-up swampland near the Shatt al-Arab. After that, there was nobody left but me. Then again, perhaps I don't count as a worker in the manner you're used to. To be precise, I was more of a...

volunteer. I just wanted to combat the stench that had swept over the sidewalks and streets and public squares since the last destruction of Basra.

Most mornings, I would be there at my usual table in a small, decrepit café, tucked away along one of the narrow walkways that led to the al-Bujarah mansion.[7] It is no different from most of the other cafes filled with the long-unemployed. Before I'd begin cleaning Um al-Burum Square of the corpses of the starved, I would sit there, in my usual place, on a thin wooden chair facing out into the street.

I'd see every last grim, glistening face – the beggars, the homeless, the blind – as they bartered away their watches and their shirt buttons, their silver teeth, or bracelets of turquoise and onyx for pieces of barley biscuits and tiny cups of bitter tea sweetened with a bit of fruit rind. Among them were artists, engineers, architects – all of whom had lost their once-effortless ability to draw, and would now probably struggle to put primary colours on a piece of paper.

They reminded me of that old story about crows who tried to copy the way that sparrows jumped from place to place. When they inevitably failed, the crows tried to return to their old way of walking, only to be unpleasantly surprised that they had forgotten how to do so.

Outside the café, there were also sellers who filled the sidewalk with technological hardware left behind in the city's wreckage: thin orange shopping cards, specially designed for the blind and elderly so they could check expiration dates and information about goods in the store; e-readers with flexible screens, either broken or badly creased; dilapidated robots that once helped people around the home, and pieces of mechanical gardeners; collapsible mobile phones with broken keyboards.

There were mixers, toasters, juicers, washers, refrigerators, microwaves. Pieces of furniture and space heaters, photocopiers and printers, televisions and curtains and irons. All of them ran on artificial intelligence, or were governed by the thin microchips lying just beneath their surfaces.

There were mirrors and bathroom fixtures, able to read the DNA of people using nearby baths or toilets, giving them complete medical checkups. Used suits, trousers and hats that could watch for illnesses and call for an ambulance at the first sign of danger, emailing medical information to the nearest hospital. Clothes that could also watch for any irregularities in heartbeats or breathing, and take 3D images of internal organs. All these things were being sold by the foreign tech traders on the side of the road at bargain prices before they hurried out of town.

Even maglev cars with cutting-edge GPS systems that once floated along on a cushion of magnetism – look at them now, strewn haphazardly on the sides of the road, coated by dust and soot. You can see them on any major road, shoved to the side, or dented and scarred by the gangs' constant brawling.

Twelve years had passed since the last great disaster robbed us of what remained of the uranium, burying the mines deep within the earth. The Shatt al-Arab dried up as well, and ever since then the people had been coming to this grand plaza hoping for their plate of rice and beans. It was the only meal for the hungry, offered once every three days – donated by the well-to-do, and distributed by the government.

I would prowl around the square, surrounded on all sides by grim, wind-whipped skyscrapers; vultures, flocks of crows, migratory storks all nesting with them. The great bell repurposed from one of the churches would ring, warning of the coming distribution of cooked rice, and the hungry families would rush forward from every dark corner, every pile of rubble, like a deluge rising from the ruined alleyways and disused metro stations.

They would make for the square, their nostrils filled with the smell of cooked food prepared in enormous vats over a low flame. They would drag their thin bodies over the torn-up concrete, with metal bowls and open mouths. They would gaze into the distance, wide eyes staring out from tattered rags; skin stretched over bone. Not one of them thought of causing any trouble, or even cutting in line, out of fear of the police officers' clubs and the butts of their rifles. That's when I'd have my chance to clean the asphalt of everything left behind to rot.

The Governor often appeared at times like this, on the giant screen suspended above the entrance to Mata'im Street. His white beard would be carefully groomed, the white hairs on his head looking they were fleeing his bald patch, which always shone in the sunlight. He would begin his usual speech, saying that Basra was not the only city facing hunger, that there were waves of violence elsewhere, that India and various African countries were still reeling from a lack of energy sources.

Everyone knew that the Governor could call on his informants at any moment; he could pull down that little periscope of his, hooked up to the internet, and sweep its lens back and forth, to see if there were even a hint of rebellion anywhere. He would watch the comings and goings of the city's denizens, weaving together scraps of information to spot any plots before they came to fruition.

Every three days, then, the people would queue up in a long, meandering line that started at the wreckage of the Al-Mina' café, in the square, and ran as far as the Mosul Bridge, in the other direction. There, by the bridge, the line broke in three.

One branch bent down to the Khandaq Creek, winding up near Dakir on the arid banks of the Shatt al-Arab. This first line snaked past the waterfront shops and the customs building, next to the main quay where the riverboat journeys to Baghdad used to launch.

The second crossed the bridge, wending its way along Malik bin Dinar Street between the ruins of the giant workshops and enormous malls that are little more than dens for rabid dogs these days.

The third turned back at the bridge to extend around what was left of the Passport Office, ending somewhere near the General Leek Bridge behind the rubble that marks the new governorate building.

I nearly always worked at night, though occasionally I'd take advantage of the people digging into their rice and beans, and begin earlier. I would drag the corpses from walkways and streets, heaping them onto the back of large carts with sturdy tires. Skeletal mules dragged these to the Basra Teaching Hospital, where fresh meat was sorted from the rotten, shrink-wrapped, and hung in giant refrigerators to send across the border that night. From there, these parcels would go on to every country in the world, for medical students to dissect and learn from.

Before this, the government had bartered away its wood, its metal, its wire and its telegraph poles in exchange for food and medical supplies; then it realised the worrying number of dogs that roamed the streets, feasting on corpses, could be turned to their advantage, and started selling them, too, to a few countries in East Asia.

Gravel and sand were another source of income, with the government exporting millions of tons to neighbouring nations – leaving much of the land around the city looking like one enormous crater, a mass grave.

The lasura trees, the cedars, a huge number of the palms – all went the same way. Who knew what the powers that be would think to sell next? *Of course, there's always the bronze of statues,* I thought, on the last morning I saw the Governor appear, as he cursed the statues from the big screen.

When I wasn't working, I loved to wander the streets of my ruined city, sometimes winding up at one of docks on the banks of the dried-up Shatt al-Arab. Or sometimes at the mass grave of automaton laborers that the government imported, years back, to replace local workers, who'd gone on strike and then been packed off to fill the prisons. Junked mechanical doctors, surgeons, musicians, artists, actors and cooks – all piled high alongside great metal bins full of smaller androids, some of them as small as spiders and flies, and long since deprived of their ability to scrub the air clean.

The graves of the plague victims – that sickness which hits the city every few years – take up wide stretches of along the river.

Yachts loll on the its banks looking like nothing so much as alien spacecraft, their amusements and outward decorations long since lost. Now they provide a refuge for homeless people and villagers displaced from the interior – preferring these shelters to the ruined towers and skyscrapers of the city, where at any moment you could be set upon by gangs of criminals, addicts or AIDS victims.

Such gangs prowl the city at night, like vampires from old-time horror films. Many of their members were the product of government commissions, cloning technology investments made some twenty years prior. Now they lived out a wretched existence, long after their designer physical attributes had deserted them. Suicide spiked among them, until the only ones left were those whose skills made them good at looting.

During my walks through these ruins – either after my work or after a feast – I would often see the young men and women being sold, in cattle markets, to foreign buyers who'd pay with things worth next to nothing – enough to slake a bit of thirst, or quiet the rumblings of an empty belly. On one occasion, I visited the covered market in Jamlun, which was lined, on all sides, by doors leading to cells where slaves spent their nights.

There, I saw one of the traders hawking his wares – a group of muscular slaves sitting on wooden benches. Their necks were chained together, and they wore thin, sleeveless shirts that exposed all the brawn they could flex.

At the same time, there were young women, all made up, sitting on the other side of the market hall. Some of them held children that were still nursing, while other children were old enough to play nearby without thinking to run away. It was as though they had already adapted to a life of slavery.

Not far from where I was watching, there was a buyer examining a beautiful girl, peering into her eyes and sniffing her mouth. Another girl next to her was holding off a different buyer, refusing to let him examine under her clothes. In the end the seller forced her to strip off her dress, and she stood there, mute, with tears in her eyes.

I would hear about cannibalism all too often, people who snatched up children and women in the dark alleys or who trapped them in the labyrinthine ruins or the deserted skyscrapers. I remember they tried it on me once, as I returned from one of my tasks. None of the kidnappers could kill me, though. Even when they tried to bite me, they were surprised at how thick my skin was, how strong my bones were, how solid my flesh was.

Their teeth broke, you see, and they cursed the hunger that had driven them to me.

Not long after the Governor turned his vitriol on the statues of the city, I was surprised one morning by somebody attempting to loop a cable around my neck. The cable was tethered to one of the Authority's giant cranes, and started to lift me up, along with my concrete plinth, high into the air above Umm al-Burum Square, then setting me down on the back of a truck. [6]

The truck drove me toward one of the great warehouses on the margins of the city. There, I found other statues in storage: one-time inhabitants of Basra, like Al-Farahidi the grammarian, the Companion Utbah bin Ghazwan, the poet al-Sayyab, Abd al-Karim Qassim and the white horse he used to ride, a copy of the Lion of Babylon with that unknown victim still beneath its paws.

I would have been cut up and sold for scrap were it not for the fact I was made of concrete – no use in that. Instead, I was shoved into a wooden box filled with straw and carried in the hold of a ship over the seas. Finally, I reached a museum that resembled a massive dumpster, where they put me on a granite pedestal next to statues of various dictators – presidents and military commanders – thinking I must be one of them. I assumed it was due to the hammer I carried.

The place was grim at night, like a cavernous prison. Nobody moved aside from the elderly janitor, whose footfalls could be heard as he cleaned the tiled floor of tissues and grime. He grumbled about this tedious work, which he could only carry out at night – by day, the place was crowded with visitors from nine in the morning until eight in the evening.

The janitor gave most care to shining the shoes of presidents and famous leaders, or to buffing the decorations on the military uniforms. He must have been the only person in the world to do so without asking for bakshish. Every time he wrapped up shining a pair of shoes, he would stand up like a soldier at attention, extending a military salute and offering his name and rank during the Third World War (some twenty years prior).

The penultimate statue he stood before was always Stalin. After he cleaned the man's shoes of all the gum and candy that the young boys stuck to them during their daytime visits, he'd turn and mimic a goose-step march down to the Hitler statue, stand before him at the ready, and give him a Nazi salute. He'd ask him about his lover Eva Braun and tell him that he was once in a relationship with a woman that resembled her.

That was before he was called up to his far-away army barracks, where he fought some other great power for control of the uranium mines – the main source of energy after the oil ran out. When he returned on home leave, he had found her in the arms of a sailor.

The young boys in the tour groups always annoy me whenever they visit – the last one was a group of children younger than ten, overseen by an olive-skinned guide who led them among the statues:

'This is Ceausescu. Look,' she said, smiling at her troupe as she lectured. 'The dictator of Romania, who was executed along with his wife Elena by secret military tribunal in 1989.'

'And this is… Hitler!' cried out one of the children. The guide turned to him excitedly, 'Yes, this is Adolf Hitler, Emperor of Nazi Germany. He waged numerous wars, and fell after he lost to the Allied Forces in 1945.'

'And where is he now?'

'He committed suicide along with his lover, then their bodies were burned according to his orders.'

Afterwards, the students moved to another leader.

'This is Franco,' said the guide, in the same schoolteacher tone. 'Francisco Franco Bahamonde, born in 1892 and died on the 20th of November, 1975. He ruled Spain from 1939 onwards, and committed a large number of crimes in the Civil War.'

'Did he commit suicide?'

'No…'

The guide had not finished speaking about Franco before some of the students hurried to another president and stood looking at him as he spoke to his friends. 'It's Saddam!'

The guide extended her approval in the same clipped tone of voice. 'Yes. He was the dictator of Iraq, ruling for more than 30 years. He led three wars, the last of which was with the United States of America, which defeated him nearly a hundred years ago. But how did you know who he was, my dear?'

The guide looked astonished when she heard the boy's reply.

'We have some pictures my great-grandfather left in our house, from when he was examining Saddam's mouth after they captured him!'

'That is… correct,' the guide followed. 'They found him hiding in a hole, 99 years ago.'

'Did they find a nuclear bomb in his mouth?'

The guide pursed her thick lips and blinked her eyes murmuring 'I have no idea! Maybe you should ask your great-grandfather.'

Notes:

1. One of the oldest public squares in present-day Basra. Originally a cemetery for inhabitants of neighbouring areas, though burial was forbidden in 1933, its name comes from 'burm,' an Iraqi word for a large pot. During the plague and famine of 1875, Hajji Muhammad Basha al-Malak – one of the notables of Basra – provided for the hungry and those fleeing sickness by setting out large numbers of such cooking pots in the square. From thence came the name 'Umm al-Burum' or 'Mother of Cooking Pots.'

2. Notable North African historian and historiographer.

3. 14th Century Moroccan historian.

4. Early 20th Century Iraqi politician and researcher.

5. The Quran forbids Muslims from drinking blood (Surah 5, ayah 3).

6. The statue of The Worker, found in Umm al-Burum Square in present-day Basra, was completed by Basran sculptor Abd al-Ridda Batour in 1970. It is intended to symbolize International Workers' Day, on May 1st, and is considered a key symbol of the Communists in Basra.

The Day By Day Mosque

Mortada Gzar

Translated by Katharine Halls

THIS VINEGAR IS EXACTLY ninety-nine years old, if the calculations I jotted down on my calendar of motivational quotes are correct, because the perfume was produced exactly a week before the enormous concrete head of Saddam Hussein hit the ground. The proverb of the day was: *The kangaroo keeps her young in her pouch, the perfumer keeps his in his nose.* The city was in chaos. The syrup factory workers were rushing home on their motorbikes, carrying empty tins that were no use to anyone and would be sold a few days later to a nursery as containers for growing carnations; as for the syrup, they'd left it oozing in the press. All of Basra was being pressed, and the syrup of agitation and anxiety was dribbling out of it; number one on the list of the top ten things being squeezed just then was the president's head under the feet of the citizenry, while the factory's syrup came in last. Numbers two to nine were large noses under angry feet.

I was sold it by one of the employees of the National Snot Bank, a rotund young man who has a nervous habit of fiddling with his collar and twitching his neck when he speaks to you. We've developed a close relationship, and he's become my agent, so I no longer need to review the bank's biannual report. He visits us and collects our snot reserves in insulated containers; the snot extraction process being highly delicate, and governed by strict legal terms and conditions, Salman Day

By spends three hours with us each time—for that is indeed his name: Salman Day By. It's said that his great-grandfather was deaf and mute as a child, and spent the hot afternoons on the banks of the Tigris (the Tigris was a small river which some theologians have speculated never existed and was in fact dreamed up by sinners, rakes and watermelon-juice drinkers). Day By Day, to use his full name, always clutched a lighter in each hand, the pockets of his dishdasha full of other, broken, lighters and his fingers ragged and torn from constantly flicking them alight. Between you and me, this great-grandfather was a simpleton nobody paid any attention to – but then he became famous in a matter of weeks when a short video of him speaking for the first time, to two American soldiers accompanied by an Iraqi interpreter, went viral.

The Day By Day clan went on to produce some of the most well-known businesspeople in the country, and amongst their descendants they count a TV presenter famous for his acerbic interviews of politicians, a gynaecologist, a pop producer, and a diminutive actor who appeared in one of Peter Spike's films (in a five-second scene showing a confrontation between two great armies in the third century BC). And here, in the heart of Basra, we have the famous Day By Day mosque, now around 70 years old. I can't imagine it will ever disappear, or its name change: the Day By Day mosque is a weighty icon in the citizenry's collective memory, and you often see it on TV as a backdrop for whichever local media personality is appearing as a guest on the BBC. It was designed by a prizewinning British architect of Iraqi origin and is shaped like a rectangle; sprouting from the top by way of minarets are two palm trees, which incline slightly towards each other such that the azan comes out in stereo – the architect of the noble Day By Day clearly wanted to play with the symbolism of unity, harmony and longevity – and now, Salman's family name no longer refers to the kid with the lighters but to these twin minarets. If he ever boasts to us, while draining our noses, of his remarkable professionalism or the bourgeois elegance and tact he brings to bear on the process of mucus extraction and storage, we don't interrupt and give him the pleasure of listening to a human with a blocked nose, we just defy him by mocking the slogan of the National Snot Bank: 'Ever tried singing with a blocked nose? It'll make you happy, lucky and rich!'

Salman is in love with his boss at the bank, a woman in her fifties responsible for drawing everyone's attention to the crook in his neck and his habit of fiddling with his collar and the second button of his shirt whenever he wants to speak: she rebuked him for it once, and kicked him out of her office, standing in the doorway as she spoke so as to be sure all the employees could hear her. After that, Salman's tic became chronic; he'd do it unconsciously once, then on purpose dozens of times, to the point he became renowned for it. And not only did his boss reject him, she also insulted him and made fun of his face and his appearance, and even his family, mocking the fact they used to sell honey, vinegar and homemade hot sauce, leaving out the great mosque and the other more illustrious facets of their history.

This is the sort of thing Salman confides to me when we sit alone in the garden. I don't like my children to hear when I'm evacuating my nose, and prefer the neighbours to listen instead: I actually *want* my neighbour to hear, as I've been trying to convince him for a long time that the sound of a man's nose is a good indicator of his health and virility. Once, Salman got so annoyed at the sight of the neighbours' heads popping up and disappearing again behind the wall that he packed up his metal containers and left, while I myself was pleasantly surprised.

Today I took out the vinegar I bought from him. The last of the children left earlier on the Euphrates train, with a warning that I mustn't go back to licking the vinegar jar, and I swore I wouldn't, knowing full well I'd slurp up a whole tablespoonful the moment he left the house, which is indeed what I did. And what a long and tedious farewell! He kept telling me I really ought to try the Euphrates train for myself, that it was so fast it would catapult him to the Gulf of Oman in just fourteen minutes, convincing passengers that the government's decision to convert the dry riverbed into a tunnel hadn't been so pointless after all. Once he'd said that, one eye on my index finger which was twirling in the air and dipping itself in imaginary vinegar, he left.

The snot is transferred from small vessels to large aluminium containers and transported north to the Gulf of Basra – the Inversion Project, which will convert south to north, is still in progress, by the way; I heard recently that workers are finding large snot reserves there, and that the project is running behind schedule: all that's been achieved on the ground is the upending of the ground, while the hardest task of all still remains, namely to work out how people will be able to walk one way when they think they're walking the other, or turn right when they're turning left, by which I mean to say that the holdup is in the psychological preparations. They're having to run opposite-direction induction workshops to train people in the new schema. Next comes the biological stage, which is slightly easier: take your stomach and your reproductive organs to your family doctor and have them perform a topical ointment massage and irrigation, and you'll soon notice your body rotating to adapt to the new orientation – or at least that's what the brochures and billboards and the posters in public toilets are promising.

Once that's all over, I'll be able to relax, and I'll stop complaining to people, and everyone will understand that I'm just a regular guy who loves the inspirational sayings written in calendars. I'm just one in a long line of employees whose responsibility over many decades has been to draw the direction of the qibla in the Day By Day Mosque (should I have mentioned that sooner?), though I know my appearance might not be that of a lowly employee of the Day By Day family – and in fact my salary comes from the government, because the mosque belongs to the Ministry of Endowments.

But first, a week of intense work lies before me, because it's me who'll be responsible for reversing the arrows which mark the qibla after the enormous earthen prayer mat on which I and two hundred million other citizens reside has been flipped back to front. That said, compared to the fish in their marble pools, who will suffer immensely as the respiratory functions of their gills are inverted, my task should be quite fun; I used to do something similar as a child, when I'd scour the walls of streets frequented by lovers, and scrutinise tree trunks in search of their arrows, the kind they draw when no-one's looking, and when I found them, scrape off their tips and make them point the other way. The fish and donkeys, with their innate sense of direction (not to mention their owners), will have a much harder time of it when their turn comes.

Salman Day By's not scheduled to come tonight, so I won't have the chance to show him I can drink an entire bottle of aged eau de toilette vinegar. Nor will I get to make fun of him for the fact his great-grandfather heard George Dubya's first speech ("Day by day, the Iraqi people are closer to freedom!") and uttered his first words – "day by day," straight from the President's lips – for two soldiers who got a kick out of poking fun at fat little boys, and in so doing became instantly famous. But all that's become a fatuous refrain I repeat to irritate him and shut him up; I ought to summon up the spirit of the retired arrow-tip chopper instead and give him a free session on how to tie his shoelaces when the new orientational system comes into force.

Baghdad Syndrome

Zhraa Alhaboby

Translated by Emre Bennett

I AM WANDERING THE streets of an unfamiliar city. At first I can't place the ancient-looking buildings – the curved city walls with their high, mullioned windows, the white slabs of a palace – but when I reach the bank of the river, the slow curving water beneath me is unmistakable. I know this city. This is the Tigris. This is Baghdad!

At that moment, a high-pitched sound rings out; I spin round but can't see where it's coming from. It calls out for me once more. It's a woman's voice, I realise: *'I can't bare the separation,'* it says. *'Come and find me.'*

As always, the dream didn't last and I woke with my heart racing and the sound of a pigeon singing at my window: 'Cokookty... Cokookty...' I rubbed my eyes and slowly got to my feet, walking towards the window in order to salute this brave creature that had made it all the way up to the 27th floor. The closest my heart got to it, however, was as I reached the edge of the window, triggering a sensor that set the blinds in motion, unfolding bit by bit, at which point the pigeon saw me and took flight.

I did this every morning: moved around the flat, as I slowly woke up, observing the whole city in a single panorama, peaking round the skyscrapers with the eyes of a child coveting what doesn't belong to him, committing to memory everything I saw, before it was too late… Baghdad.

This is why I lived in the centre of this bustling city, in this modest tower, among much taller ones. I was happy to get a place from which I could view the whole city, district by district; I lived in Karkh and could see Resafa on the opposite bank of the Tigris. My parents were appalled at the rent I was paying, called it extortionate, but for me it was more than just rent I was paying.

The dream that kept returning each night was trying to tell me something, I knew: a countdown had begun, ticking off the days until my life would change. Despite learning to expect this dream, each night, the experience of having it was always shocking. I'd wake up wanting to contact the special helpline, but what could I tell them about the dream that I hadn't already? What could the robot on the other end know about how I felt? In the past they'd committed me to a special care unit for mental health patients suffering from textbook symptoms of 'Baghdad Syndrome'. But I'd escaped knowing that in my heart, despite everything, I was what they called 'a smiley person'!

I quickly put my clothes on. It was Thursday morning and I had to get to work. On the round, green table in the middle of the sitting room, I had left a kettle of cold tea; I quickly poured some into an estikan, took a swig, then abandoned it, and started inspecting the pile of letters stacked neatly in front of me. I ignored the letter with my name printed rudely along the top – *Patient Sudra Sen Sumer* – followed by a summary of a recent set of results. I ignored the letters addressed to 'The Centre of Care'. Instead I picked out the files addressed to 'Architect Sudra Sen Sumer', and those related to the square that I had been commissioned to design.

I descended in the elevator, surrounded by the puffy faces of the half-slept, and smiled to myself as I greeted my vehicle, parked in the first space at the front of the building.

The space had been reserved for those with special needs, which I didn't have at that time, but who can say no to the luxury of such a convenient, permanently reserved parking space in the middle of a crowded city? This could very well be the last space going. Lack of parking space is what drives so many workers to invest and live in the newer, residential cities around Baghdad – which is also where my parents live.

Arriving at my office, I greeted this person and that person. I promised so-and-so I would spend an evening with him, and someone else insisted I started visiting him daily. The morning passed with a mixture of other such pleasantries and work. At noon, my colleague Utu accompanied me to the square that I had to create a design for.

The square was on the Resafa side; a long stretch of land reaching along the bank of the Tigris close to Gilgamesh Street – or 'Abu Nuwas Street', as my granddad called it, the way he always accidentally referred to places by their old names – the bookshops on 'Al-Mutanabbi Street', the shops in 'Karradah', or the restaurants in 'Mansour'. Utu and I stood and examined the dimensions of the space and considered what might be possible for it. The decision wasn't easy, as the theme of the commission was a well-trodden territory – the mythic past – explored by countless architects and sculptors before us, with their statues of Mesopotamian kings, Gilgamesh and Enkidu, the Code of Hammurabi, the Hanging Gardens, or the Winged Bulls.

I stood and imagined a different kind of design – a tribute to someone that wasn't famous at all, perhaps a monument representing a Sumerian doctor, highlighting another side of this civilisation...

Utu cut off my train of thought by murmuring something to himself that I couldn't make out.

'Share your thoughts with me,' I said.

'It's nothing... ,' he replied at first. 'I just feel... that I'm betraying my people by being here changing this square.' He seemed embarrassed by what he was saying. Perhaps he saw then the sudden change in my expression as I struggled to process his reply.

'Well… I think that we are finished here,' he added with a smile. I suggested that we walk a little to the front where a series of restaurants served fish fried in a particular way, passed down through generations. They grilled the fresh fish after cutting it from its back and sticking it on stakes in front of flaming wood.

I would treat myself to this 'Mesguf fish' whenever I felt oppressed by work or tired of the canned and frozen food that my mother would supply me with each time I visited. Utu apologised for not taking me up on my offer and went to his obligatory weekly dinner with his family.

I decided against eating there on my own, and contacted my niece, Ishtar, who was at her private secondary school in some street near the four-storey Bridge of Mesopotamia. I invited her to join me once her classes had ended.

Perhaps it's not the most exciting thing for a teenage girl – to be asked to go eat fish with her uncle – and she complained instantly about the walk, and suggested other non-fish options instead. She soon warmed up, though, when she found out that I was mainly meeting to share my thoughts with her on the square. Ishtar's eyes glimmered, as she sat down to eat with me: 'I can't wait to tell my friends that my uncle is creating the new design for Lovers' Square,' she exclaimed. The name 'Lovers' Square' was not unfamiliar to me; I knew the old tale behind it.

It was said that the square was a place where a sculpture of two lovers had stood from time immemorial, and that one day the two lovers had simply vanished without trace, causing many people to mourn and curse the circumstances that would drive two lovers, even sculpted ones, out of Baghdad. The place had remained empty in honour of their love, ever since. Other cities around the world have exploited this idea, some of them replicated the statue exactly, others dedicated parks and squares of their own to the two lovers, offering them a haven to arrive at. It seemed that Ishtar and her friends had all heard of this story, and the rest of the world's relationship to it, but, to me, the square represented just another project. Despite this, and without regarding the story as anything more than a sentimental myth, I felt passionate about this project. I knew that it might be the last piece of work my eyes would see.

I returned to my flat in the evening to spend the rest of my day alone. I followed the news for a bit, then spent some time returning calls. Most importantly, I ignored the letters on the table regarding 'Baghdad Syndrome' until, finally, I retired to my room and gave myself up to sleep and the dream that haunted me.

Once again I find myself wandering the streets of a city that appears to be Baghdad, with the cries of that woman in my ears: *'I can't bear the separation... Come and find me!'* But this time it's different; this time she doesn't stop there.
'The night of the separation was black. This hand, which wiped away my tears, is no longer my hand! Black, it's black and my nights are black!'

I woke up terrified. I stumbled to my feet and began pacing around in a corner of my flat, reassuring myself that the black the woman in the dream spoke of hadn't taken me yet: I still had my eyesight.

My heart racing, I made my way towards the pile of letters about 'Baghdad Syndrome', despite already knowing most of their contents.

Baghdad Syndrome — a phenomenon whose exact causes are still the subject of considerable genetic and medical research — is characterised by a small number of key symptoms, including an irregular heartbeat and a seemingly arbitrary subclinical depression, measurable through neurotransmitter activity and other indicators in the blood. Despite the evidence for the depression, patients remain largely 'smiley' – that is to say, sociable, active, emotionally balanced, and free of typical depressive behaviour.

Ultimately, sufferers – who are often between the ages of 30 and 40 – succumb to complete blindness, which is preceded by a period of waking hallucination, in turn preceded by unusual nightmares. The syndrome takes its name from the city that has so far produced the majority of diagnosed cases. Experts are currently trying to make a connection between the condition and the prolonged exposure of our ancestors to toxic substances a century ago. However, even now, the exact nature of the substance is unknown. All that is known is that there is a spontaneous DNA mutation found in all patients, although the position of this mutation on the gene map varies from person to person.

Each gene sequence starts mutating after birth and continues up until the blindness phase; consequently it is often difficult to detect early enough to advise against reproduction. Diagnosis is possible, however, before symptoms become manifest, and wide-spread screening in infancy is currently being proposed: so as to provide future sufferers with priority opportunities in education and work, as well as treatment and special provisions, to help them cope with the condition and the complete visual loss.

I knew all this, but they still attached the booklets to every letter, as they knew I hadn't used the contact number they'd given me. I was aware that the gene was inside me, changing at an accelerated rate. I knew that soon my vision would start to go the way the lights once did over Baghdad all those years ago.

When the dreams began I consulted my doctor; she said that it was a sign that the blindness phase was nearing, and recommended I see a specialist quickly. That was what I was resisting.

I stared at the address on the leaflet and was close to giving in, but managed to postpone it one more time, fearing it would prevent me from enjoying my family gathering that Friday.

Friday came and I went to visit my parents, with my brother and sister's families all visiting as well. The time passed quickly with conversation, laughter, real tea and large helpings of my mum's signature dish. When it was over, my brother surprised me by taking me to one side and presenting me with an early birthday present. He couldn't wait another month, and wanted to see my face as I opened the box in front of him. I was delighted and surprised but instantly trembled on seeing what it was. Inside the box was a sculpted forearm. It looked almost heroic, all black and marble-like, and, while I didn't think it was, the arm reminded me of the lady's hand from my dream.

'Don't you see how awesome it is!' my brother exclaimed. 'You're mad for these sculptures, aren't you?... I pulled a lot of strings to get this, believe me...'

'It looks like an artifact, how did you come across it?' I asked, trying to collect myself.

'The black market, my dear boy! Nothing is impossible,' he beamed.

'As much as I like it,' I confessed, 'I'm not comfortable with the fact that you bought it from a thief, or at least someone who bought it from a thief... Maybe we should just hand it in to the Museum.'

A wave of disappointment crashed over my brother's face, who launched into his defence: 'I bought it, I paid good money for it – that's what's important here. Even if it isn't a genuine piece, the Museum isn't going to say, 'Oh you take it, we don't need it.''

I didn't want to hurt my brother, or expose my true feelings towards this present of his, so I took it and tried to think more rationally about the whole thing.

Once back in my flat, I unwrapped and inspected it. Despite feeling strangely possessive over it, I still intended on taking it to the Museum. I struggled to recall why exactly it reminded me of the dream... The woman had talked about a hand and blackness, and here was a black hand which my brother had bought from the black market... This is an omen of the on-coming darkness of Baghdad Syndrome, I thought to myself, then chided myself: the syndrome is limited to psychological effects, not coincidences! I haven't dreamt of this hand before now!

When my fear subsided, I put down the thing that was supposed to be a hallucination, and went to bed, awaiting more sentences to be added.

I can't bear the separation... Come and find me...

The night of the separation was black. This hand, which wiped away my tears, is no longer my hand! Black, it's black and my nights are black...

I've wept for so long and no one has wiped away my tears, unless you count the tears of heaven that have washed my cheeks, and maybe one other who watches me as I weep...

The ring that he wanted for her hand is too small for my finger and I'm not his love, and he's not my lover...

My body is the story of a woman who flouted the restrictions, who fled and now pleas to return — so that she can tell her king the story of the thousands of nights, of the tens of decades...

I woke panicking. It took me an hour or more to get back to sleep, and when eventually I did, the dream returned once more. By the morning I had lost all composure. I felt as if every new event was a sign that I would now turn blind, and that I stood on the edge of insanity.

When I couldn't find a way out of my train of thought, I decided to embrace it all, and search for the identity of the woman in my dreams.

I phoned in sick at work and typed out the sentences in full, so I didn't forget them. I prepared a few things, including the Kleecha cookies that my mum, who hoarded them, kept me in constant supply of. I set up three hologram-screens on the wall in front of me and began my search.

I didn't know what I would ask the search engine; the first thing was to work my brain. I had to accept that the woman would not leave me alone unless I found her, and that the arm my brother had given me was in some way a message from her.

I scanned the black forearm searching for a clue, but found nothing. The base of it, severed just above the elbow, suggested the arm was in a bent position, and must have been cut from the left side of the original statue.

Despite all this, I didn't know where to search and soon became exhausted by the whole process. I stretched out on my bed and tried to relax enough to sleep. If she invaded my peace once more, she would at least bring me another sentence.

'Don't leave me weeping forever.'

She was guiding me towards her with this sentence. I went back to the holograms that I had set up in my office. I entered the sentence into the search engine which instantly produced thousands of results, all adding to my confusion. I changed the search to 'images' and there were even more results than before. One of the pictures, however, stopped me.

Unlike the countless other images melodramatically conveying themes of love and separation, this picture was of a sculpture of a woman standing serenely, with her arm raised, in front of a man, sitting listening to her. They both wore old fashioned clothes. I clicked through to the page and learned that the photograph came from a University outside of Iraq. Attached to it was a poem.

I felt disappointed as the page didn't lead back to Iraq. After looking carefully at the picture, though, I was certain it was from this city and that the forearm of the sculpture in the photograph resembled the one that had been gifted to me. I also realized that the setting of the statue was very similar in dimensions to Lovers' Square.

I read the poem; the language was difficult to unpack but the pain flowing from it was undoubtedly real.

The last line of the poem read: 'And you, Scheherazade, will remain weeping forever.' Evidently the woman who had been stalking me each night was Scheherazade, herself. I started some basic research into the author of the poem.

She was an Iraqi writer: born over a hundred years ago into a well established Baghdad family. Her father had been taken from her, by government security forces, while she was still a child, never to return. Her mother died in an air raid during the war that ousted that regime. She lived a real life story of star-crossed lovers until her husband was killed for belonging to a different religious sect to her. After that, living as she did in an area populated by her husband's sect, she had no choice but to flee in the middle of the night, with her child. She left all her clothes and possessions behind, all her worldly goods, and abandoned her country to seek peace in another. However, Iraq never abandoned her and she continued writing short stories, which she always signed with the sentence: 'And you, Scheherazade, will remain weeping forever' – the last thing she remembered from her home city.

Just as I arrived at this information there was a knock at the door. My niece, Ishtar, stood at the entrance: 'Uncle, tell me you're okay so I can ring your sister and reassure her!' she blurted. I laughed before inviting her inside. She explained that my sister's friend, who worked at my office, had told her that I hadn't turned up for work that day, and that she had tried ringing me to no avail; so she sent her daughter to see if I was okay.

Even when I'd managed to forget about the Syndrome, everyone else conspired to remind me.

I picked up my phone to find more than ten missed calls from my sister and twenty from my mum. The phone started ringing in my hand; it was Utu asking about me.

'I'm fine, I'm working on the square design from home today,' I told him before he'd had a chance to speak. 'Actually, since you're there, tell me: what do you know about the monument that used to stand on the site?'

'There was a monument of Scheherazade and Shahryar… Shahryar was some ancient king who killed each one of his wives the day he married them, so they couldn't be unfaithful to him. He married and killed a thousand; but then he married the daughter of his minister, Scheherazade, and couldn't kill her because she played with his mind, telling him a story each night which she wouldn't complete until the next day. It was a book, or a film or something…' Utu paused. 'Why do you ask?'

'This may sound suspect, but… Scheherazade is following me,' I explained.

'You need some rest my friend…' Utu replied. Then, under his breath: 'The emigrants dream of returning but they never return.' The phone cut out.

When Ishtar heard what I'd said to Utu she got scared. 'Uncle… don't you think you should have a talk with mum?' she asked.

'Is it urgent?'

'I heard you talk to your friend about a stalker… Scheher… Schehera… I didn't catch the name.'

'Her name is Scheherazade… you know the name of Lovers' Square but you don't know the name of the lovers in it,' I laughed. 'Look, I'm fine. There's just a small matter that confuses me.' Then an idea struck me. 'Actually you *can* help. You're better with technology than me. How do you feel about staying a few hours and helping me? I'll ring your mum and tell her that I can drop you back tonight.' Then I added: 'We can order take out from any restaurant you want.'

'Oh uncle,' she replied, 'if it's to do with Lovers' Square, you don't even need to ask!'

I told Ishtar about all that had happened to me, about the dream and the mystery of the statue's hand coming into my possession, about discovering this early 21st century author. All this drew Ishtar in and we both started building upwards from this.

Ishtar and I tried getting the names of the author's descendants but the city's online genealogy archive only went back three or four generations, and none of them seemed connected to her.'

I couldn't find a way of getting to the author's relatives to link, in any obvious way, to me or to the ancient figure of Scheherazade. Nor could I find a copy of *1001 Nights*, which I now knew was a very ancient text, to fathom any clues from its plots.

We attempted to use the official government data-port that holds specific threads for every citizen, starting with their births and recording all subsequent life events; but this proved useless, as the system only reached so far back. At one point Ishtar thought of searching the regional archives knowing that, in the olden days, people would meet at established places for socialising, and subsequently exchange photographs of these meetings through online networks that were called 'social media'. These sites were no longer available, but after a few private calls I was able to obtain a large archive of random images of social websites from the archives. I managed to access these by claiming they were needed for my design research; so my professional practice was now being exploited by Baghdad Syndrome!

I was sent a folder of photographs showing people who participated in establishing the site and the various dates involved. However, the names were blurred and unclear due to the low quality of photography back then.

We tried giving the photographs a resolution-boost to make them clearer, and with this, we were able to sort the images into groups. Clearly these people cared about the statue, and considered it a symbol of Baghdad, but what we found perplexed us. The statue didn't just disappear overnight as the story about the Square claimed; it was more gradual, people must have simply not noticed this as they so distracted by other events.

In one set of pictures the statue is missing a forearm, in a later batch both arms, and in the third group Scheherazade is minus a head, and in a fourth set Shahryar is there alone, listening to no-one. I stared at this groups of pictures.

'Uncle look!' Ishtar said, interrupting my thoughts. 'There's an earlier set, with the statue intact... And here's a close-up of Scheherazade's face ... and, if you look, you can see fine white lines, or scratches, running down her black cheeks... These lines... they look like tears!'

I looked at the pictures and she was right. There were tears streaming down Scheherazade's face.

I was certain that the tears on Scheherazade's face were somehow connected to the author and her migration from Baghdad, as the appearance of the tears happened around the same time. I then returned to the task of searching for the author's descendents. Ishtar proved invaluable here, as she downloaded an app onto my system that used faces of people from the past to find contemporary descendants.

I uploaded a picture of the author and her partner and immediately received algorithm-estimates of what her children and grandchildren might look like, which were then matched with contemporary records. Initially, I doubted the process greatly; all the matches were with people living outside Iraq and still used names that seemed ancient compared to contemporary Iraqi names. Then I realised that she and her family never returned to Iraq, so proceeded to email three of her alleged grandchildren.

Ishtar and I had a break, ate a little and discussed her studies, but my mind remained on the mission. I was nearly finished when I jumped at the sound of an email alert.

The first reply was from a grandson confirming his relation to the author but confessing he didn't know anything about a statue. Likewise from the second. The granddaughter then replied saying she had once heard her grandmother tell a story about a statue with a scratched face. She also said she knew nothing of the loss of the statue's hands and head.

I went back to the start, pulled up the photographs again, and tried to think about the bigger picture. Ishtar and I pored over them again, one by one, and slowly the obvious dawned on us.

The pictures that showed Scheherazade's tears dated from immediately after the poem was first published. It was the author who had scratched those tears on the stature, before writing that Scheherazade would remain weeping, and then abandoning her, and her city, to cry.

Then came the first photo in which she'd lost her left arm. This was not the usual selfie of lovers or teenagers posing in the square, with the statue in the background; this was a different type of selfie, of a military person, with an ancient piece of weaponry round his neck. He appeared to be waving at the statue – as if bidding it goodbye after performing some great service to it. In all the pictures from this set, Scheherazade could be seen, in the background, surrounded by chaos, smoke rising in the sky above her, people scrambling for cover. This led me to suspect that her hand must have been stolen in this chaos, by thieves, and what it must feel like to have part of you owned by one of them, for the hand not to be her hand any longer.

With that I felt that I had an explanation for two of the sentences from my dream, the tears and the left hand. A few sentences still remained vague as we tried to connect each of them to the remaining pictures and arrange them:

> *The night of the separation was black. This hand, which wiped away my tears, is no longer my hand! Black, it's black and my nights are black…*

— We pulled out this sentence and attached it to a photo in which Scheherazade's left arm, the one gifted to me, was missing.

After that:

> *I've wept for so long and no one has wiped away my tears, unless you count the tears of heaven that have washed my cheeks, and maybe one other who watches me as I weep…*

— We attached to a headless picture.

Lastly:

> *My body is the story of a woman who flouted the restrictions, who fled and now pleas to return — so that she can tell her king the story of the thousands of nights, of the tens of decades…*

— was attached to the picture where she is both headless and without arms. One sentence was still missing though.

In the photos where Scheherazade had only lost one arm, our attention was drawn to the repeated appearance of a young man and woman in the foreground. We ordered these images chronologically but could find nothing but happiness in their expressions. In another picture, the man seemed to have been inspired to decorate the statue as he waited for her, to surprise her. Another photo showed the place filled with smoke.

The following group of photographs were the headless ones. The severed neck was hard to look at. Shahryar couldn't have cut her head off, the way he threatened to in the story, but there was another person in the background of several of these photos. An old man.

None of the photos were taken for the old man's benefit it seemed, he was never centre stage. And Ishtar downloaded another program to search all the photos for any other appearances, in the archive. It seemed he appeared in many of them, not interacting with the main people in the photos, but sitting on his own, in the background staring up at Scheherazade's face. He only stopped appearing in them after the head was removed.

After the head disappeared, the number of photos of the square reduced sharply. Most of the images from this time showed groups of women around the decapitated statue; peace, it seemed, had been restored to the background city. Shortly after this, Shahryar and the remains of Scheherazade disappeared altogether. Despite the progress we'd made, connecting the faces in the pictures to names of people now living in Baghdad was extremely difficult. Hiding links to the past was very common back then. Old names and surnames became dangerous things to hold onto, and people were allocated new, neutral names, free from any affiliations to religions or sects of the past. The slogan we read about in history was: 'Leave behind your names and live!'

Every generation yearns for the past. The father says that his time was the best. The grandfather says that *his* was the best. This leaves us forever romanticising the past and singing its praises until we find ourselves reliving it; this is why we ended up bearing the same names and surnames we used five thousand years before. The cycle had to be broken. So our history teacher told us.

The following day I excused myself from work. Downloading a list of names and addresses, I left the house in pursuit of any information that would guide me back to Scheherazade.

I had with me downloads of the images, in the hope they might mean something to those descendants I'd managed to trace. The first dozen or so addresses I visited, I left disappointed, knowing nothing more about their ancestors or their connection to the square. I was starting to doubt the whole project.

I returned to my flat and threw myself onto the bed. Once more, I was haunted by the same dream, but for the first time I woke without panicking. I knew for certain it was guiding me. No longer was it merely a nightmare painted on the walls of my mind by Baghdad Syndrome. I took an official leave from work and continued my door to door investigations for three further days until I had answers.

That young man, in the early photos, had planned to propose to the woman he was often seen with – there, under the statue. He arranged everything, even decorated the square. But he never managed to place the ring on his darling's finger. On her way to their rendezvous, just a street away, she had been caught by a car-bomb, and had lost her right arm. After this, she refused the marriage and fled with her family to the North. With this, the young man broke off Scheherazade's right arm and placed the ring on its finger. He married his cousin and the hand remained with him as a reminder of the severed love. The ring stayed on the hand for many decades – completing an unlikely broken treasure that later owners would never appreciate – until eventually it became detached, and was lost.

As for the old man, he turned out to be a famous sculptor who, in that corner of the square, found a place to watch Baghdad. When the author came to scratch the tears onto Scheherazade's face, she told him her story. The sculptor remained there, depressed, watching the events unfold around Scheherazade until he could no longer bear the sight of her weeping alone, without anyone to console. So he removed the head and took it home.

The head remained safe, hidden among the many sculptures of his own that his family inherited.

As for the women seen gathered around the statue in its final years, these represented an Iraqi women's rights association, who couldn't bear seeing her stand there in front of Shahryar helpless, enslaved, and beheaded. They produced slogans demanding the restoration of the remains for the dignity of all Iraqi women, and when these went unheard they conspired to remove the remains of Scheherazade's body and continued to protect the statue for so long that they forgot it wasn't actually theirs.

Within a few weeks, I had managed to locate all the pieces of Scheherazade but failed to track down Shahryar. The search had cost my sanity dearly, however; I had lost all sight of the design I was supposed to be working on for the square. It was as if Scheherazade had told me stories that I couldn't ignore and I needed to return to her place each day to listen.

Then one night the final piece arrived. I had popped out to get some take-away biryani from a nearby restaurant and returned to eat it in my flat, before phoning the office for an extension on the design deadline. As I dozed I heard her voice again:

My lover is closer than you can imagine. The migrants dream of returning but they never return. My lover, however, didn't emigrate and he isn't a migrant.

Her words spun through my thoughts, and made contacting Utu my first priority the next morning. I passed the window without even glancing at Baghdad, and that morning's tea sat untouched as I went to call him.

'Where can I find Shahryar, Utu? I need to find him!'

'Sudra,' he sounded like he was about to laugh. 'You have become obsessed with Scheherazade. I'm afraid your symptoms have intensified.'

'Scheherazade has charged me with finding for Shahryar; I can't return her statue to the yard on her own. I don't want to go blind before I do this.' Utu sighed and fell silent for a few seconds. Then suddenly he spoke: 'There is a gathering. Of the old families. You should come. My family will be there.'

The day of the gathering arrived, and though I was full of anticipation I hadn't forgotten that this was going to be the first time I met Utu's family. I left early to shop for some sweets to take with me. I made my way to the location and found that it was a family-run, private club, hidden away in the back alleys of old Baghdad, surrounded by date palm trees. The door was locked so I called Utu and I soon heard him unlocking a series of inner doors for me. Eventually the outer door swung open and shocked me with what it revealed.

In the middle of the spacious inner hall sat Shahryar. Men, women and children were gathered around him talking, laughing and playing. I stood there dazed, not quite processing what I was seeing.

A group of men approached me with Utu among them: 'None of us have forgotten the names of our ancestors – be it the fourth or fifth generation,' Utu explained. 'My great-grandfather's name, on my father's father's side, was Ali,' one of the men said. 'My grandfather's on my mother's side was Omar,' another said. 'My paternal great-uncle was named after Jesus,' a third man added. 'My mother's father was Azzad,' said a fourth. 'Sarkis', said another. 'Yashar.' 'Seth.'

The names went on and on, until Utu concluded: 'All of them were lecturers and friends at Baghdad University. They were worried for Shahryar, afraid that he would become dishonoured and would fall from being a king to a mere customer in this new world, that he would be accused of disloyalty to the country, not being an Iraqi.

And yet Shahryar has witnessed all the blues of the Tigris, all its reds and its blacks; its floods and its draughts. The men had succeeded in keeping him hidden, to be returned only when Scheherazade returned. You see, if you're a sufferer of Baghdad Syndrome, you know that nothing has ever driven us, or our ancestors, quite as much as the syndrome of loving Baghdad.

A year on and here I stand, between Scheherazade and Shahryar in a square on the bank of the Tigris. I cannot see her but it's as if I can hear her telling him stories – stories of the thousands of nights that they were separated for. Stories that fill the air, along with the sound of the pigeons fluttering above our heads, singing, 'Cokookty... Cokookty...'

Operation Daniel

Khalid Kaki

Translated by Adam Talib

DISTRICT: KIRKUK (GAO'S FLAME), 2103.

It was still early when the SMS bracelet around Rashid's wrist vibrated, waking him. The message was brief and precise.

Dear Beneficiary no. RBS89:
    Good Benefit.
    Today, the first Saturday of the month, is dedicated to 'eradicating the remnants of evil.' The Beloved Units will be mobilised throughout the city between the hours of 9am and 6pm. Anyone in possession of audio or audio-visual recordings of the re-classified languages (laser on titanium or carbon fibre) should turn these in to the officially designated droids patrolling immediately. Anyone failing to comply with these instructions will be arrested and promptly archived.
    Gao Dong, The Beloved, Loves You.

There was nothing unusual about these messages, not since the Venerable Benefactor, Gao Dong, who currently preferred the title 'The Beloved', had made the Memory Office his priority department. For those who don't follow State politics, the Memory Office is both a security and social service. It functions as a security service by virtue of its core mission: to protect the state's present from the threat of the past. But what makes it a social service, you ask. This stems from the intimate relationship the government has with its followers, trainees, and admirers – not exactly the relationship between superior and subordinates, rather benefactor and beneficiaries. That was the touch of genius the Venerable Benefactor had brought to all areas of life in the black-gold state of Kirkuk, 35 years ago. What he did to protect them all from the threat of the past was itself a service. For instance, he had re-classified all the city's older languages, the most ancient of which dated back 5,000 years, as 'prohibited'. As beneficiaries, the people were forbidden from speaking Syriac, Arabic, Kurdish, Turkmen, or any language other than Chinese. The punishment for speaking those languages, or reading about history, literature, or art *in* them was merciless: you were archived. This involved being incinerated in a special device – resembling one of those UV tanning beds that were all the rage in the late 20th century – your ashes would then be removed to a facility that produced synthetic diamonds, where, just a few hours later, all that had been left of you would re-emerge as a tiny, glittering stone. It was called 'archiving' because a crystal can store an infinite library of information locked in its chambers – more secrets than the House of Wisdom – even a traitor's personal history could be preserved in them. (It was something to do with electrons and vibrations.) Once polished, these crystals would be sent to another factory where they would come to adorn one of the Benefactor Gao Dong's shoes, or one of his many hats.

Rashid didn't possess any recordings in any of the languages Gao Dong wanted to strip Kirkuk of, but he spoke three of them fluently. This he couldn't deny. He'd learnt them from his parents, and he knew something in his bones would compel him to teach them, in turn, to his own children one day, if he had any. But that's all he felt about the issue. He was no rebel. He knew there were some people who would fight, or even die, for these languages, claiming they held the key to citizens' real hearts. But these were just rumours Rashid had heard. He'd never met one of these rebels.

A few days earlier a special search-and-raid unit had turned up several discs and tapes, dating back 80 years, on a hillside in Daquq. Information had been leaked by a double agent to the search unit who reported that the artefacts were found to be full of songs – songs that some people in Kirkuk had heard *about*, but that no-one had actually heard. According to the gossip, these had been among the most beautiful, exquisite pieces ever recorded. Songs about the singer's beloved and the pain of being separated from her; songs about the beauty of nature and the women who go down to the village spring to get water, and lots of other things like that. The times they lived in sounded much simpler, safer and more humane, than our present age.

The discs and tapes were immediately destroyed and a written and verbal order announcing the enforced surrender of all similar material was issued. Everyone in the search unit was transferred to a 'training session' in the city's Great Hall of Benefits. Things like this seemed to happen every two or three weeks. They'd be digging in search of water and come across some old computers; the digger's claw would scrape against old computer parts or a glimmer of tapes and discs would peek through the disturbed earth. Some people were prepared to pay a lot of money to get their hands on that sort of rubbish – despite the threat of being archived – and several people had already been transformed into little square-cuts for being in possession of 'found' music or films, which now graced one of Gao Dong's waistcoats and lapels. Whenever Rashid thought about the Benefactor's love of fine costumes, the collars and sashes, the cravats and cummerbunds, he couldn't stop another image from entering his head: that of a gag. It was because of a slogan he had heard once, or read: 'History is a hostage, but it will bite through the gag you tie around its mouth, bite through and still be heard.'

The time was nearing 13, and the young man, in his twenties, who called himself 'Rashid', considered going out for the day. If he stepped out into the street, he would automatically become 'Beneficiary no. RBS89' – or 'RBS' for short (the number '89' simply referred to the year he was born). But if he stayed in, he could remain unnamed, no-one. Under the rule of Gao Dong – who'd come to power in the wealthy City-State of Kirkuk as a result of the Three Month War in 2078 – all citizens had been reclassified as beneficiaries. This was because everything His Excellency now did for them, or to them, or on their behalf, in his governmental and military capacity as commander and chief, was to their benefit. His security measures were for their benefit; his purges of camps outside Kirkuk, driving out refugees wanting to share in their spoils, was for their benefit; his war on worker's unions and their terrorists – all for their benefit. And every citizen prayed for his continued protection, of course.

This is how things stand in Kirkuk today – or rather in what the Beloved Commander calls 'Gao's Flame' – in honour of the city's eternal flame.[1] The old districts of the city and the Assyrian Citadel look more or less as they have done for over a century, even though the city has been cut off from Mesopotamia for four decades now, since Gao Dong's arrival; the outskirts of the city have been developed as the city has expanded, and outside them are the camps, the migrants, and exiled union extremists. Over the years, Gao's Flame has grown as one of the world's richest City-States, a place of enormous wealth and investment, thanks to its petroleum reserves, where its citizens enjoyed peace and tranquility. An Assyrian from the city, named Sargon, built the Citadel anew and in each of its seven corners he placed huge gates flanked by winged bulls in the style of those sculpted by the Gods of Arrapha[2] thousands of years before. Although the Three Month War had damaged parts of the aluminium-clad Citadel wall, the bulls still preserved their timeless lustre, shining in the sunlight, and staring out into each coming day with dark, wide eyes, their strong, youthful hooves planted firmly into Arrapha's soil.

In the evenings, the young man known as RBS89 – or 'Rashid Bin Suleiman' to his family – would meet some friends outside the Citadel at the Prophet Daniel Gate; from there, they would go to the ruined graveyards nearby, to chat and catch up before dusk became night. In the graveyard, some of his friends – not *him*, of course – would sing songs in the old tongues and recite poems that Gao Dong's government had specifically reclassified. It was as though these friends were performing some secret ritual, something like a religious ceremony, even though the songs' lyrics were completely domestic in their subject matter. They had never told Rashid – so he could never be accused of knowing – but these friends had all lost parents and relatives in the Great Benefactor's arrival – hundreds had been executed by Gao Dong and his purification policies. His friends would sing these simple love songs in hushed, ardent voices, heedless of the danger they faced if the authorities overheard them. 'The people of Kirkuk had fallen into Gao Dong's grasp as easily as a butterfly into the hands of a collector,' his friends would say, 'because the whole world had changed. The balance of power had tipped towards China, and now Kirkuk, once a solitary kingdom, speaking entirely its own language,[3] had become just another outpost.'

One evening, about three weeks before, as the young men and women had gathered in the graveyard, a red government droid hovered towards them. His friends knew what to do, switching seamlessly from the ancient song they were singing at the time, to a Chinese one. They always managed to have a contemporary Chinese song ready, whose melody matched exactly with the ancient one. This was standard procedure whenever a member of the red police came near, and it worked every time. 'I wish I were a stone / At the base of the citadel,' they would sing one minute, 'So that I could be friends / With everyone who visits.' Then, a second later it would be love song set in modern Beijing. It was a cat-and-mouse game. But listening to them sing that first song, they all sometimes wondered, privately, if something was missing, if something at the core had been stolen away, and if the now they inhabited was impenetrable to it. Whatever it was, it could no longer reach through; instead they all mouthed a set of sounds they didn't truly understand.

One of the young men gathered there that evening – there is no evidence it was Rashid – failed to follow the normal procedure. While his friends switched effortlessly to a Chinese pop song, this particular youth carried on singing in Arabic, or possibly Turkmen. Indeed he sang louder and louder as the droid came near, inspecting him close-up. He drowned out the singing of the others, many of whom broke away quickly and disappeared. The words were obviously strange to him:

There are three fig trees growing
Beside the wall at the citadel.

But he kept singing them, as if singing them louder and louder would give them more meaning, somehow, or help their meaning reach through to him:

My hands are bound,
A chain is wrapped around my neck.

Don't yank the chains,
'cause my arms already hurt.

Three weeks later, the afternoon that Rashid received the bracelet text, he decided against going out. It was a Saturday after all, he didn't need to do anything. Instead he would play with his artifacts. These were not recordings, you understand; they contained no written or spoken or musical examples of reclassified languages. They were merely sculptural objects, with interesting shapes – glittering discs or dull cuboids with spindles of tape inside.

By some strange coincidence, Rashid owned hundreds of them, and also had the means to duplicate them – just as objects, of course, for their aesthetic, sculptural value. He was stood in his pyjamas, scanning his shelves, trying to decide which one to play with, when a special detachment of red droids burst through the front door to his house, brushing aside Suleiman Senior, and marching up to his room. Some people have claimed that RBS89 managed to take one of these objects and extract a melody from it, in the time the droids took to break down his door. There is no evidence to support this, nor the claim that RBS89 was singing this melody as he was carried away, or that he danced in his prison cell, singing the same. Similar rumours were spread about the other suspects removed by red forces in the Begler, Piryadi, and Azadi neighbourhoods, in the crackdown that became known as 'Operation Daniel'.

Even more unfounded is the superstition, circulated in some of the poorer districts, that a melody sung in the face of death resounds louder in that palace of final destination, the glittering Archive. That would imply that when General Woo Shang presented Gao Dong, The Beloved, three weeks later, with a new pair of diamond-studded boots, in his castle on the Euphrates River, one of the tiny gemstones on those boots would still be vibrating, deep inside, with the words of a silly song – 'Take me to the bar./ Take me to the coffeehouse. / Let's go somewhere fun...'[4] This is not true.

Notes

1. A gas flame in the middle of the Baba Gurgur oil field, near the city of Kirkuk, and 16 kilometres north-west of Arrapha; it was the first such field to be discovered in Northern Iraq by Westerners in 1927. The field is 40 metres in diameter and has been burning for 2,500 years. It was considered the largest oil field in the world until the discovery of the Ghawar field in Saudi Arabia in 1948.

2. Arrapha or Arrapkha was an ancient city in what today is northeastern Iraq, on the site of the modern city of Kirkuk. It began as a city of the Gutian people, became Hurrian, and was an Assyrian city during most of its occupation.

3. Around 2150 BC, Kirkuk became occupied by 'language isolate' speaking Zagros Mountains dwellers known, to the Semitic and Sumerian Mesopotamians, as the 'Gutian' people. Arraphkha was the capital of the short lived Guti kingdom (Gutium), before it was destroyed and the Gutians driven from Mesopotamia by the Neo-Sumerian Empire c. 2090 BC.

4. Lines from 'Near the Citadel' – a popular, early 20th century Turkmen song, of anonymous composition.

Kuszib

Hassan Abdulrazzak

UR WAS SUPER EXCITED. His boss wasn't known for generosity, so the day he offered him two free tickets to the Feast, Ur could barely contain himself. 'I have to be in another sector this weekend,' his boss explained in his usual, ridiculous baritone. Ur suspected a new mistress.

He couldn't wait to get home. 'Guess what sugarlump?' he called out to his wife. 'We're going to the Feast!' Ona's eyes lit up for the first time in months.

Ur knew that Ona was unhappy with their move to Sector 42, even though they lived in its most exciting city, Centre Point. She never came out and said as much, but some resentments take a long time to simmer, even longer to bubble and froth.

The tickets in Ur's hand felt like the first sign of the better life he had promised Ona. The annual Feast was the place to be at that time of year. Impossible to get invited to, it offered everything: a chance to sample the Sector's finest gastronomical delights; the opportunity to mix with the cream of society; and introductions to the kind of people you'd never normally encounter as a mere sorting clerk, which is what Ur was. A sorting clerk with big ambitions.

'We have access to the fashion show as well!' Ur declared. He kissed Ona, tasting oregano and basil on her tongue before sampling, with the tip of a spoon, the sauce she was preparing. They tried to make love that night but it proved, as on previous occasions since the move to Sector 42, to be a joyless affair. Later, in the early hours, Ona sat up in bed and began sobbing quietly to herself. Ur pretended to be asleep.

The morning of the Feast finally arrived, and Ur took Ona shopping. They treated themselves to tailored outfits, the type they'd never dream of buying normally, then, while Ona booked herself into a beauty salon, Ur killed an hour staring at window displays of laser-harpoons. On returning home they showered, perfumed and dressed. Ur thought Ona was looking very attractive in her new outfit. He put his arm around her but she gently pulled away as she fixed her earrings. Ur's faint smile disappeared. He wondered whether over the course of this night things would get better or worse between them.

Ur parked the Paradigm Hover in the vehicle dock, and the couple took the magnet capsule to Alliance City Station (in a part of town that used to be called Revolution City in the old days). From there they reached the exhibition complex on disposable solar-blades, which they kicked off and recycled in a terror-proof bin in front of the complex. Through the glass façade, they could see the Feast was already underway.

Passing through the main entrance, Ur and Ona held their invitations aloft, to be scanned by the security system. As each invite was read, the mesh of lasers criss-crossing the doorway disappeared and the guest walked through. On the other side, Ona and Ur were met by a pair of ten-foot high robotic puppies bounding towards them, enthusiastically. The puppies bathed them in purple light emitted from their big, adorable eyes as they scanned for weapons. Ur had to remind himself that cute as these floppy-eared, chrome-coloured puppies were, they were designed to pounce and swallow terrorists whole, in a fraction of a second. Bombs could explode noiselessly inside their stomachs.

The great hall took the breath of anyone who entered it. Using reflective surfaces and synthetic-crystal paint, the designers managed to convey a sense of vastness, even infinity.

Row upon row of stalls stretched like waves over an

ocean. Farmers and merchants from all over Sector 42, not just Centre Point but further afield, were gathered to display their produce. The first fifty or so rows were dedicated solely to wine.

Ona paused in front of one stall that displayed wines with peculiar-looking labels. The labels featured a painting of a farmhouse surrounded by horses and fields stretching into the distance. It was like a picture out of an infobite manual. Ur asked the old merchant manning the stall if they could sample some of it. The merchant poured two generous glassfuls and handed them over.

'Smell it first,' he suggested to Ur who was about to down it in one go.

'Why?'

'That's how it was done in the old days'.

Ur sniffed and was pleasantly surprised, even moderately aroused, by the aroma. Ona followed suit and a smile stole across her face.

'Now drink,' the old merchant instructed.

Ur began to drink. The wine caressed his throat like a sheet of velvet. Seconds later, an explosion of taste erupted in the back of his throat. The alcohol reached the brain and he felt his muscles relax with a substantial quantity of happiness.

'This is not normal wine, is it? What's it made of?'

'Grapes' replied the merchant.

'Grapes?'

'Red grapes to be precise. This is how they made wine here in the old days. We are the only company that has been granted a licence to create produce according to the old ways'.

'But this tastes great,' Ona interjected. Ur and the merchant looked at her surprised, assuming she hadn't been following their conversation. 'There should be more things like this. We should be encouraged to learn about the old days.' Ona's voice was ripe with enthusiasm. The old merchant poured another shot of wine for her then leaned forward to whisper, 'You know, the elders frown on this, madam.'

Ur finished his sample and asked: 'Does your company produce any normal wines?'

'Sure. Here try this.'

The merchant took out a container from the 37 degrees incubator and poured a sample in a fresh cup.

It was local wine with the usual two rivers logo on the label.

Ur tasted the wine. It was the familiar sort, the type he could obtain easily at his local market. He formulated his next question carefully, before asking with confidence:

'What kind of humans is this made out of?'

'It's from the blood of locals,' the old merchant replied in a lacklustre voice, clearly unimpressed with Ur's rather unrefined question.

'Perhaps you should be asking, rather, what they were fed on?' he suggested.

'Er, yes, precisely,' Ur blushed.

'We prefer organic methods. That's what our company is all about' The merchant's hands animated his speech. 'So for a start we cook their meals. Most wine merchants don't bother with such details. Humans can indeed eat raw meat, but their teeth are not particularly suited for it so they prefer cooked food'.

'Just like us!' Ona yelped.

'Yes, perhaps there is a degree of similarity with us.'

The merchant produced more wine bottles with different logos. 'These come from further afield. Have a taste'. He poured fresh glasses for the couple.

'What do you cook for them?' Ona asked with real interest, as cooking was one of the things she excelled at.

'Whatever we can get cheaply: sheep, donkeys, rats, that sort of thing. Sometimes we feed them their own babies but we found it best not to make them aware of that, otherwise they get agitated.'

Ona put her glass down. Ur took another sip from his.

'We screen them for disease on a regular basis. They're

susceptible to so many viruses, as a species. We have to be careful especially when handling their fluids: blood, mucus, semen, etc. Most of their viruses can not cross over to us but we still have to follow regulations.'

'Well you have a good produce here. It's high quality,' Ur said this knowing what the merchant would ask next.

'Would you like to purchase anything, sir? We can have it sent to your address.'

Before he had time to reply or fumble for his credit chip, Ona interjected.

'Maybe later, there is still so much to see.'

She was always the sensible one. Ur also knew that by saying this she was reminding him of their plan: To work in Centre Point until they'd saved enough credit to buy a plot of sea back home.

They sampled more wine from other regions. Mainly made from human blood, although the 'Other Vinos' section offered vintages derived from dog, cat, hamster, and pig. Ona was getting a little tipsy. Ur kissed her. She kissed him back and he could feel a flicker of fire between them. *But not enough*, he thought. The blood on their lips intermingled. Her brown-eyed African mixed with his German blond.

After the wine, came the meat stalls. To Ona it seemed that every part of the human was used in one way or another. There were arms, torsos and thighs hanging from hooks and several counters displayed heads stuffed with fried tomatoes or peppers where the eyes used to be. At Ona's local market human meat was often highly processed and vacuum-wrapped. It was easy to forget where it came from. But here she was confronted by the entirety of the human animal. Ur passed one head with two carrots sticking out of its ears. He had to suppress an attack of the giggles as he made his way forward.

Then there were the sausages; coils and coils of them, stacked ancient castle walls in refrigerated trays. Ur knew these were made from things like ground-up eyes, lips, cheeks, tongues, muscle, spinal cord. Just about every part of the human anatomy fed into those cylindrical delights. Ona picked one of 'the foreskin and herb' coated sausages to examine it when she noticed a crowd had gathered around a small platform directly opposite her.

It appeared a demonstration was about to take place. The butcher standing on the platform was dressed in orange overalls. On a table in front of him lay an entire human leg. The tanned limb was completely smooth unlike many others that hung around them. Something about it suggested femininity. The toenails were painted red and the middle toe was adorned with a tiny silver ring. The butcher stood with one hand firmly gripping the thigh; with his other hand he held up an old-fashioned cleaver, its edge glinting like a laser beam. Once a sufficient crowd gathered, he raised the leg and cleared his throat, then for a moment he stopped himself, noticing the toe ring. With a flick of the cleaver it was gone, flying through the air above them, then landing somewhere behind him with a tiny jingle. The nail on the toe also came off and a small trickle of congealed blood dribbled over the other toes and onto the table. Ur, Ona and most of the others watching recognised that the leg was organic; real fresh.

'The most important thing you've got to realise when making sausages is that the finished product is only as good as the ingredients it contains.' The butcher's voice bellowed, silencing the few who were still engaged in conversation. 'The meat must be fresh.' He paused to let that point sink in. 'It must also be high quality and have the proper lean-to-fat ratio. It's no good using overweight specimens for this, which is why farmers who know what they are doing, make sure their stock receive plenty of exercise. You give a human half a chance and he'll just sit around doing nothing.' Laughter erupted at that last comment. The butcher didn't smile. 'That's not good. A fat human makes for a poor sausage indeed.'

He then raised his meat cleaver high above his head and brought it down with enough force to cut a round portion of the upper thigh. He picked up the chunk of meat and held it forward. It was now inches away from Ona's terrified face. 'See! No fat on this one. She's a beauty. And look at the colour, it's just marvellous.' Ur was nodding in agreement. The majority of humans from Centre Point were beautifully sun kissed, making their meat particularly tasty. The butcher flung the meat into a solar-powered grinder.

'The temperature of the meat should be kept as cold as possible during the grinding and mixing. This grinder is kept at a constant four degrees and can be flicked into self sterilizing mode when not in use. The low temperature keeps any nasty human germs from being active. Later, the meat is cured with a mixture of anti-bacterial and anti-viral formulations before stuffing into hog casings. Any questions so far?'

'Yeah, I have a question,' a youngster shouted from the back. 'Why is there such a big price difference between the sausages?'

The butcher lodged his cleaver in the middle of the leg and said, 'It's to do with the *type* of meat. Humans come in all varieties: black, brown, pink, yellow. This determines the flavour but also those of us from Sectors one to twenty have taste buds that pick up other qualities. Scientists now think that what the human was thinking or feeling at the moment before processing can affect the quality of the meat.'

A feminine voice announced through concealed speakers: 'Will guests with tickets to the fashion show please proceed to the Inferno Hall. Take the gravity elevators down to 7/8.'

The gravity elevator was a huge round platform rimmed with unconnected metal bars and studded with hovering rubber poles. Through the gaps in the metal bars the guests, including Ur and Ona, entered, and were told to hang onto the poles suspended in mid air. The platform then descended slowly through a shaft that doubled as a giant, cylindrical aquarium. Ona gasped at the beauty of the scene that encased them: a multitude of brilliantly-coloured fish gliding in perfect formation like hover jets in traffic, yet capable, at a moment's notice, of changing direction. A school of them can break away with a twist and a jerk reminiscent of a limb twitching in sleep. Humans had lived in the midst of this beauty but failed to appreciate it. This was one of the points discussed at length in a government document called 'The Moral Case for Sector 42 Invasion' which everyone had been sent. Standing there, knowing she would not be able to describe the beauty of these fish, she wondered how anyone would be able prove or disprove human appreciation of anything. Maybe that document had overlooked this point deliberately.

Ona thought of the lessons she received at the fundament before leaving for Sector 42. Most people moving to the Sector for work, including Ur, didn't bother going on such courses, but she wanted to learn about the place she would have to call home for a while. Amongst the things they debated at the fundament was the question of whether humans had a civilisation. This question cropped up regularly and was hotly contested. She remembers her professor explaining that whilst humans *themselves* considered their system of co-habitation to constitute a civilisation or, even more bizarrely, a series of civilisations separated by time and/ or geography, this wasn't proof of anything. Just because native beings think something is true does not make it so, the professor explained. After all, their art was repetitive; their science laughably limited and they had very little respect for one another and least of all to the globe where they lived. 'No,' the professor argued, 'you can call it what you like but civilisation it was not.'

At the time, Ona had been troubled that some of the implied failings of humanity could also be found in her Sector. But whenever she tried to raise this point, she was told that human failings were of much greater magnitude and moral repugnancy. The decision to invade, taken by the Elders of Sectors One to Three, was not made lightly, she was constantly assured, and there was ample documentation for her to pour through, if she wanted, to reassure herself about the reasoning behind it. Every time she tried, however, the endless stream of dry reports and hearings sent her quickly to sleep.

'What was surprising is that humans failed to grasp the inevitability of their defeat,' the professor said. 'They actually put up a fight!' This didn't happen immediately because when the Alliance forces first arrived they picked Centre Point as their first base, which took many by surprise. Centre Point was a city that humans referred to as *Baggy-Dad* (the natives may pronounce it differently, the professor said as an aside). Humans in the elite Western and Eastern flanks of Sector 42 were particularly surprised, indeed insulted, that it was not one of their own cities that had been occupied first. They had always imagined – very repetitively, through their so-called 'art' – that this would ultimately be the case in what they called a 'space invasion'. And their 'intellectuals' speculated wildly on why *Baggy-Dad* was picked above cities such as *Newey Pork* or *Lindon* or *Beige-inn*. Was it location? Climate? Geography? Or the fact that *Baggy-Dad* was already war-torn and its inhabitants weary of fighting that attracted the 'aliens' to it?

Here Ona remembers her professor digressing. 'It's funny the words humans used to refer to us. In one of their dominant languages they describe us as 'aliens', a horrid term. Whereas humans in Centre Point who spoke *Arabaic*, call us '*ka-in-at-fatha-i-ya*' or something similar sounding which meant 'space creatures', an arguably more neutral term. Of course, what they should have called us, based on logic if nothing else, was their betters. I mean how hard is it to work out that having crossed vast distances to reach this Sector, we are the superior race technologically, and therefore their betters? But then humans were never that good at logic.' Something about this argument had struck Ona as suspect but before she'd had time to formulate what exactly, the professor had moved on to the next point.

When *Baggy-Dad* was first colonised, humans in the rest of Sector 42 were alarmed, but not to the point of taking decisive action. All too soon they learnt that, unlike a virus outbreak or a rampaging fanatical armed group, this threat could not be ignored for very long. *Baggy-Dad* proved to be an excellent base for the Alliance from which to spread north, south, east and west, conquering the entire Sector in a relatively short space of time. What was odd, the professor pointed out, was that humans eventually organised an activity they called 'resistance'. It was the only time that all flavours of humans: pink, black, brown and yellow united for a common purpose. This flicker of intelligence came far too late, however, and ultimately it was easy to defeat humans by making deals with some of their more powerful members. It is rumoured that a select few who collaborated with the Alliance were spared slavery and subjugation. It is not clear where these exceptions are living now. Some say they were teleported to the caves of Sector 3078. The names of human cities and districts were quickly changed on all available maps so that they were at once made familiar to the Alliance and disorientating for the natives. Hence places like Revolution City, a short lived hub of resistance, became Alliance City.

Ur was also lost in thought, as the gravity elevator continued to descend through it's aquarium–sleeve. But he wasn't contemplating the history of Sector 42. He was rather thinking about his job instead. Sorting clerks such as himself were needed after the change (or 'the invasion' as some humans irritatingly referred to it) to catalogue everything. Throw out the useless, keep what was relevant to the Alliance and most importantly destroy all remnants of so-called '*human culture*' that could give rise to another resistance. *It's amazing,* Ur thought. *How one can carry out as complex a task as a change of an entire Sector with the absolute minimum of knowledge?* Ur consulted databases that gave him the information he needed to catalogue, but he rarely had to dig deep into the details. There simply was no time to be thorough, considering the volume of work. Occasionally the databases had some missing information and Ur would have to activate Protocol 7 in order to investigate the item he was cataloguing, using information that humans themselves had kept about it. This was generally discouraged and a sorting clerk could not activate Protocol 7 more than three times in any given work cycle. Otherwise alarms would sound with the higher-ups. Once Ur had come across a book made out of something called 'paper'. It carried a drawing on the front of a bald human with a huge white collar, looking apprehensively at the viewer. The information on this particular human was very sketchy and nowhere near as detailed as say the entries on anatomy books that were of particular interests to chefs working for the Alliance.

Ur was able to find out that this male wrote words that humans kept repeating for centuries, often on a stage, for the 'entertainment' of other humans. This illustrated handsomely the point often made about the limitation of human art and its inherently repetitive nature. Yet as Ur went through the book, he found the stories oddly compelling, despite their often preposterous and primitive plots, made perhaps even more intriguing by the fog of a double translation (Ur was deciphering the book – which had been translated into Arabaic from its original language – with the aid of an interpretation device). Linguistic opacity notwithstanding, he found himself laughing at a macabre joke in one of these stories about a human trying to avenge the murder of the male that gave rise to him, but procrastinating over the act in odd and elaborate ways. Everyone in the sorting chamber where Ur worked turned to look at him in surprise that day, as he struggled to stifle his laughter. To compose himself, Ur reminded himself of how pathetically humans had failed to work out the basics of intergalactic space flight, driving back his momentary fascination with the book and restoring his old feelings of revulsion towards these creatures. It was only when this feeling of superiority had a *physical* manifestation

– a shudder of revulsion – that balance to his psyche was restored.

Such a crisis never happened again and Ur made excellent progress in his work. What he wanted more than anything was to be promoted to Head of Filing. Tonight was his chance to further that ambition, if he could only make the right contacts.

These were his thoughts as the gravity elevator continued to descend. Then, finally, one of the fish caught his eye. Its colours and its strange movements infiltrated his most private thoughts. He looked over at Ona and wondered about the cause of their unhappiness. What if he actually *were* promoted? What then? Maybe they'd save enough credit and return to Sector three sooner. Would that restore the desire they'd once felt for each other? Their relationship felt empty; he was at a loss to explain it. All he knew was that it was causing them both tremendous pain.

The platform reached level 7/8. The guests walked through a wide, dimly-lit corridor which opened onto the cavernous space of the Inferno Hall. At the back of the hall stood a stage, and Ona and Ur made their way towards it. A light-show had already begun, accompanied by loud music. They were seated at a table along with several other couples. Ur realised they had found their way to a particularly exclusive area of the hall, as everyone around looked impeccably well turned out. Of course this would be the case, he thought, as the tickets belonged to his boss who was constantly socialising to further his career. Models were parading the latest winter collection on stage including a coat made out of sheep hair (what humans called 'woollen'). The buttons on the coat were made from chemically-preserved, steel-reinforced human fingers. *An elegant design*, thought Ur. Ona, however, looked ashen-faced as she stared at the models, though Ur would never have noticed in the low lighting.

He spotted some of the other guests reaching for a jar from the set placed at the centre of each table. They were fishing things out with thin steel forks and placing them in their mouths as their bodies bobbed up and down in time to the music. Ur glanced at the couple next to him. The male looked familiar. He decided to take a chance, and break the ice with some of these higher-ups. A chance like this doesn't come every day. He leaned over to the male sitting next to him and pointing at the content of the jar in front of them asked: 'What are these?' The male answered but Ur couldn't hear him over the music. He cupped his ear and said, 'Say that again.' The male shouted in his ear. 'Oh, OK.' Ur's eyes lit up. It suddenly dawned on him that the male was none other than the Chief Archivist, responsible for firing and hiring all heads of filing. Ur smiled meekly and said, 'I've never tried these before.' He picked up the fork in front of him and plunged it into the jar. He had to fish around until the teeth of his fork bit into their prey. He pulled out his catch and popped it into his mouth. 'Mmm. Zingy!' he declared as if his approval of the food could win the Chief Archivist's favour.

Ona was always less daring when it came to trying new food. She whispered to Ur, 'What is it Ur?'

'It's a foetus, sugarlump. They're a delicacy. You must try them.'

Ona's face clouded over. She looked at the other guests, munching away at these small human creatures, and realised that these foetuses could not have been farmed in such quantities unless they had been both germinated and aborted by artificial means. On the stage, a gorgeous female from Sector one was modelling a Spring dress made from stitched-together nipples. Ona suddenly felt nauseous. 'I need to cleanse.' She got up from the table and began to walk quickly. 'Wait Ona…' Ur shouted. Then, when everyone at the table including the Chief Archivist turned to look at him, he smiled meekly to suggest that it was nothing, of course.

Ona looked for the sign for the cleansing chamber then quickly crossed the hall towards it. Ur didn't know what to do. Should he stay and continue socialising with the Chief

Archivist or go see to his wife? In the end, he excused himself and left the table, his pace increasing the further he got away from them. In fact, once out of sight and safely down the corridor that led to the cleansing chamber, Ur broke into a run. Ona couldn't wait for him. She wasn't even sure if she wanted him around right then. The dimly-lit corridor stretched out for an eternity. There were bars, shops and clubs on either side. Other doors had no signs and it wasn't obvious what they led to. Finally Ona reached the cleansing chamber and once inside lowered her head into a basin. Her skull labia opened and undigested food, mixed with urine, erupted in thick ejaculations. Ur walked in and steadied her by holding onto her neck with one hand and her short tail with the other. 'Let it all out,' he said. When her skull closed again, Ur ran the tap to wash off any remaining traces of vomit on the top of her head. He then dried her with some paper napkins.

'Leave me alone,' she said as she pushed him away.

'What's wrong?'

'I hate this place.'

'We can leave if you want. I think the exit is this —'

'I hate this Sector. I hate it. I hate it. I hate it.'

'Hey.... hey, calm down.'

'We should never have come here. We were happy back home. We just got greedy because of the salary they were offering you and didn't stop to think, not for one milicount, about these poor creatures. I can't bear to think what we've done to them. I mean eating their unborn? Really, Ur?'

It took Ur a few seconds to realise what Ona was talking about and what had upset her.

'They're just humans, sugarlump.'

'I know they're just humans but they have feelings, don't they?'

'I suppose.'

'It's wrong, Ur. And we're being punished for what we are doing to them. This is why it's no good... it's no good between us anymore.'

Ur had always found Ona's belief in the 'Setter of the Cosmological Constant', with his powers to punish and reward, endearingly anachronistic but right then it irritated him immensely. Still, he was determined to placate her.

'Sugarlump...' Ur tried to hug Ona but she pushed him away with even greater vigour than before.

'Stop calling me that. It's such a stupid word.'

Ur was hurt. 'But sugar is the most important fuel for all organisms in all the know –'

'I don't give a shitlump!' Ona interrupted. Ur reached out to her and once again she rejected him.

'I can't stand you touching me anymore.'

Ur was beginning to panic. He'd never seen Ona so agitated before. So he stood still until her breathing slowed. His mind drifted towards the Chief Archivist. There was still time for them to return, apologise for their sudden departure, blame it on Ona's delicate stomach and resume the conversation that could, if he played it right, lead to that promotion. But Ona said, 'I'm not going back into the Inferno Hall, Ur. No way'. Ur struggled to believe he had come so close to achieving his goal, only for it to be swept away by something as trivial as a foetus. Then, as he looked at Ona, a pang of guilt swept through him like electricity and he was ashamed of his naked ambition. Finally he said, 'It's alright. But lets at least get a drink before we leave; I spotted a bar down the corridor when I was running after you. It looked quiet.' Ona didn't reply or even nod but the look she gave him was no longer hostile.

He walked down the corridor and she walked a few paces behind him. Halfway towards the bar someone called out to them.

'Hey... youhoo... yes, you... come in, come in.'

A door had opened. A door that Ur could have sworn was previously closed.

'Come in... don't be afraid... that's it. Come in.'

Ur and Ona walked through the door. The room was a

small bar. It could not seat more than half a dozen people. It glowed with a soft blue light, giving the effect of a moon-lit night in a rural part of Sector 42. Blue light also came through the opaque surface of the bar. Behind the counter stood a tall, dark, semi-naked, heavily made-up…

'Hermaphrodite!' Ur said this out loud then instantly regretted it.

'That's right sweetheart. "Kuszib" is the name and bartending is the game. What's up sugar? Is that sweet little thing your 'Mrs'? Mrs… what a strange little native word.'

'I've read about you,' Ur said in the same, hypnotised voice he had uttered the word 'hermaphrodite.'

'Oh I do hope it was suitably scandalous.'

'I don't mean you, specifically. I mean about your kind.'

'My "kind"? Do you mean bartenders? You must be a discerning business traveller who reads all those hoity-toity journals.'

'You are from Sector Nine. The only place where conditions allowed highly evolved hermaphrodites to dominate.'

'Allowed!' The hermaphrodite rolled the word over its tongue. 'No one "allows" anything in this universe, sugar. Shit happens because shit *can* happen.'

'Or because the Setter wills it,' Ona interjected.

'Oh, you're so cute,' Kuszib said patting her on the head then turning to Ur: 'Can I keep her?'

Ur was still hypnotised.

'Something the matter, sugar?' Kuszib inquired.

'Sorry, it's just I've never met your kind before.'

'Your kind, your kind, your kind!' snapped the hermaphrodite. 'You are not too kind, gentle sir, for harping on "my kind".'

'Come again?'

'Oh surely,' and with that the hermaphrodite began to rub one of its tentacles until it hardened then it inserted it into an orifice located beneath its left nipple.

'Ohhhhh.... That's fucking gooooood!'

Ona giggled. 'Ur, is he...?'

'Yes darling,' Ur replied meekly.

'Did he just ...orga?'

'Not yet, my lady.' The hermaphrodite interrupted. 'Ohhhhhh. Yeaaaaaaa.' Then, talking to its thrusting tentacle: 'That's it space cowboy. Ride it. Oh yes, yes, yes. There. That's it. That's the spot. Oh right there... there... no... a little to the left.'

The tentacle, one of three protruding out of the hermaphrodite's navel, swayed to the left and began to pound the sub-nipple orifice with great vigour.

'Ride it. Ride it. Ride it! Ride it you big love barnacle.'

Shouting and screaming, the hermaphrodite knocked several bottles neatly arranged on the glass shelves behind it with its two arms and two free tentacles, while its body shuddered like a spaceship crashing through an event horizon.

Ona placed her hand over her mouth to stop laughing but the laughter seeped through nonetheless. Ur was feeling very uncomfortable. 'We should leave,' he suggested.

The hermaphrodite grabbed hold of Ur's right wrist and began to squeeze.

'No. No. No. I'm nearly there. Wait. Wait. Let me just look at you both. Ahhhhhhhhhhhhhh.... There it is. YES! It's all over. Thank you. Thank you so much. That's the best one I've had all day.' Without letting go of Ur's wrist, the hermaphrodite shook Ona's hand and simultaneously wiped its brow with a napkin using one of its tentacles.

'I'm "Kuszib" by the way,' the hermaphrodite said, forgetting it had told them. 'The best bartender this side of the Milky Way.'

'What an unusual name you have,' said Ona.

'Glad you noticed, hun. I gave it to myself. Like a treat. I didn't like my old name so I thought why not have a name-makeover? And let it be exotic. When in doubt, go exotic, that's what I always say. To be honest I've never said that but it sounds like the sort of thing I would say.'

'Does it mean anything, "Kus-what"?' asked Ur.

'Kus*zib*. It's *Arabaic*.'

'It's the language of the natives of Centre Point,' Ona explained.

'I know!' Ur snapped, irritated both by Ona presuming he didn't and by the memory of the book that had unsettled him in the sorting chamber flashing in his mind.

'If you must know,' Kuszib said, nonchalantly. '"Kus" means.... well no point beating about the bush, it means "cunt". And "zib" means "cock". Put them together and you get: me! Lovely really. What are your names?"

'Ur' said Ur 'and this is my wife…'

'Ona,' said Ona.

'Ur and Ona. I am in your debt. I don't know what it is about you but you just got my tentacles all tingly. Let me pour you a drink. It's on me. Kuszib always rewards those who reward her.'

'Her?' Ur said with an unintended tone of incredulity.

'Only on the weekend. It's easier to get laid that way,' Kuszib said with a grin.

'Now don't tell me you two have been sampling that swillpiss they're serving upstairs?' Kuszib reached for a bottle of wine from under the counter and placed it before the couple.

'Some of it was good,' Ur protested.

'Whatever,' Kuszib rolled her eyes. 'You're really married to this putz?' she asked Ona.

Ona just looked bewildered.

'A male who knows nothing of good wine shall never, in all his years, pleasure a female…. even I, a larker in the land between, know that.'

'What?' said Ur.

'Glad you didn't ask me to "come again",' Kuszib said and winked at Ona who resumed giggling afresh.

'Your wife knows what I'm talking about. I can see it in her eyes though she's trying to hide it.'

Ona fell silent. She looked at Ur who didn't meet her gaze.

Kuszib's tongue snapped out of its mouth with tremendous speed. It wedged deep into the cork of the wine bottle and, with a sharp, elegant pull, uncorked it. The room filled with a bewildering aroma.

'Ommm.... Inhale. Inhale my lovelies. Inhale!' with eyes closed, Kuszib's nostrils began flaring and vibrating in a struggle to capture every last molecule of its vapour.

'Now drink!' Kuszib ordered, pouring them two large measures.

Ur and Ona did as instructed. Their taste buds danced to the music of the wine, their cheeks filled with blood, their heads with joy, and their limbs floated on an ocean of invisible feathers. This was the best wine they had ever tasted.

'What is it made of?' asked Ur.

'It's a secret' whispered Kuszib. 'But hang around long enough and you might find out'.

'I better stop, it's making me..' Ur was feeling unsteady. 'Ona we shouldn't… we have… a long… long… way to get home.'

Kuszib placed the back of its hand against its forehead and with a theatrical tilt of the head said, 'I do not wish to greet the world with sober eyes.' Then looking directly at Ur: 'For sobriety is the virtue of the rankest pedant.'

'Who… who said that?' Ur asked earnestly.

'I did, mother-fucker. Now drink up. That goes for you too sweet giggle-fits.'

With a nervous giggle, Ona finished her drink. Ur also downed the rest of his wine. Kuszib filled both of their cups.

Ur opened his mouth to speak. 'Hush!' the great hermaphrodite commanded.

The couple stood frozen, not daring to break the silence.

'I sense trouble' – Kuszib said, with her eyes flicking between Ur and Ona – 'in this union.'

'We really must leave,' Ur said in a tone so unassertive, it sounded like a plea. But then he glanced at Ona, and she was mesmerised. It is as if Kuszib spoke to the core of her being.

Kuszib's hands reached out to the couple and turned them so they faced each other. Using her tentacles, she poured more wine into the cups and placed them against their lips.

'Drink.'

The couple did as instructed.

'Now close your eyes.'

With eyes closed, they downed the wine Kuszib was offering them. 'Time for a rare slice from the very same source as this wild nectar,' Kuszib said as she slipped two sausage wafers into their mouths.

The meat tasted like... like... like... how very odd, thought Ur... how very peculiar, thought Ona... it tasted like... falling in love all over again.

★

This is what they experienced:

Fog. Thick fog. Neither had ever seen fog before. It did not exist in Sector three. They thought they were looking at a white screen but one that was slowly beginning to fragment and reveal... what?

Sand. Hot, white, smooth sand.

And they were running on air, just millimetres above this ocean of sand. Their bare feet occasionally brushing against the surface grains of this great desert.

Ur looked at Ona and saw a beautiful, naked, young human female. Ona in turn looked at her husband and saw a handsome, naked, young human male. Although they had turned into humans... in this vision... in this dream... they were still Ona and Ur. 'But who do these bodies belong to? What are their names?' they both wondered.

The next thing they knew they were running towards some unknown destination in the distance. They headed East – towards the land of the yellow-flavoured humans, their century-old towers deserted and crumbling, then they crossed an ocean, their feet lightly gliding over the foam of the waves, to the land of the chubby, predominantly white-flavoured humans, now kept captive on huge prairie farms, where they were mercilessly exercised to lose that excess fat. Then they crossed another ocean, dipping south to reach the landmass where the few remaining black-flavoured humans dwelt, almost extinct because their flesh tasted so good, and because sustainable farming laws had been implemented too late. Instead of running back to Centre Point, Ur and Ona took a detour. They headed north to the continent where the best wine, made according to the old ways was manufactured. Now they were running across dewy grass and wild flowers, their feet firmly treading on the ground. Ur stretched his hand out to Ona and she did the same. Their fingers touched then parted then touched again as they continued running. Their breathing was growing heavy but tiredness did not set in their limbs. They were that rare creature, that creature on the verge of extinction: a wild human. Being a wild human in Sector 42 meant that you were constantly on the run.

They reached a farmhouse. It was abandoned. Beyond it several horses stood munching on grass in a field stretching out to the horizon behind. The eerie silence of the place made the couple feel exposed. They pushed at the door of the farmhouse and found it unlocked. Once inside, they tried to catch their breath, Ona let out one of her characteristic giggles. Ur grabbed her and they kissed. Shortly after, Ona stretched out against the dust-covered wooden floor of the farmhouse. Ur opened her legs. He was taken back by the beauty of her sex, its complexity of intriguing folds and moist flesh. And when he approached for a closer inspection, its smell bewitched him. It had a similar aroma to the wine Kuszib had served them.

Ur realised that his sex organ, his human tentacle, was now erect with excitement. He had somehow expected this reaction but was surprised to find his lips and tongue were also prickling with anticipation. He kissed Ona's feet, her calves, her thighs, turned her over and kissed the soft flesh of her buttocks, then turned her again to kiss her lower outer lips. She began to moan and the sound of her moans excited him further. His kisses turned more frantic and involved his tongue, lips, even teeth – used sparingly, not to hurt, but simply to suggest the possibility of danger.

'So this is how humans mate,' Ur whispered erotically in Ona's ears. He was surprised at the sophistication of their pre-love. For him, Ona's body became like the terrain of some strange Sector, full of variety and intriguing little details: the texture of the navel, the softness of the belly, the round smoothness of the breasts capped with solid, dark concentrations of flesh, particularly pleasing to his tongue. Ona reached for his tentacle and brought it closer to her sex. She looked up at Ur and remembered a photograph in the infobite manual that had shown two humans mating in this very same position. But it was one thing to read about the invaded, it was quiet another to become them, Ona suddenly realised. When Ur entered, her cheeks filled with blood.

Kuszib fed them with more slices of sausage.

They became lost in sexual love. Both could sense that the end was nearing, that their brains were making their way towards an explosive event, something approaching a sensual supernova.

A few seconds short of orga, Ona sensed they were being watched. But before she had a chance to look over Ur's shoulder, her heart was penetrated by a harpoon.

Hunters from Sector three had been watching them through a window and waiting for them to approach but not achieve orga. Just before reaching that zenith, the harpoon had pierced Ur's back, skewered his chest, passed through Ona's heart and lodged firmly in the wooden boards beneath them.

The hunters burst quickly into the farmhouse brandishing knives. Two of them lifted up the bodies by the hair on their heads, whilst others proceeded to slit their throats and collect the precious wine in special caskets they'd brought with them. This was the wine of wild humans caught in the act of love, making it the ultimate aphrodisiac. After the blood was drained, the only task left was to chop up the bodies, collect the meat and process it for sausage making.

★

Ur was the first to open his eyes. He could see a multitude of slimy tentacles had emerged from his own nipples and were sliding over, writhing with and penetrating Ona's outstretched tentacles that ended in thorny receptacle cups. Ona opened her eyes and for the first time in months Ur could see true desire in them. They continued to make love for several hours as Kuszib fed them with wine and meat gathered from the corpses of wild lovers.

When they awoke the next day, not able to recollect when and how sleep had befallen them, the couple found themselves back in the vast white hall. All the stalls had been removed, and their two entwined bodies had been left undisturbed in a now empty desert. Ona and Ur emerged from the glass building, hand in hand, feeling relieved to have survived their strangest night in Sector 42.

On quiet days, Ona would think about the two lovers whose bodies they had inhabited that night and whose names they never knew. She felt sorry for them but concluded, in the end, that what mattered was her happiness and if that had to be revived by the blood and flesh of human lovers then so be it. Love is the hardest thing to sustain. Even humans, in their day, must have known that.

The Here and Now Prison

Jalal Hasan

Translated by Max Weiss

MR. FARHAN RAISED HIS eyes and gave everyone in the room a stern look.

'So, kids...'

He was allowed to call his students 'kids'. To them, he must have looked as old as Noah.

'What do we call this?'

With his thumb, he clicked a button he was holding, and the youthful faces became transfixed as the classroom rebooted, then powered up as a primeval forest with trickling streams and singing birds. A lion came into view, growing larger and larger, until it took up an entire wall.

'A lion,' they replied, largely in unison, realising he was still waiting for an answer.

'And what do we call this...?'

He clicked again and a different lion appeared, this time leaping gracefully through a blazing ring of fire in a circus tent crammed with spectators.

'Another lion...' they groaned, knowing where this was going.

The teacher rubbed his palm with his thumb as if trying to burrow a hole through it. 'Don't you see? This is one of our conundrums. The lion is a 'lion', the street is a 'street',' he made quote marks in the air, with his fingers that clearly his students didn't understand, 'and so too with the world. We call it the world whether it is our own world or that which we no longer know, the way it was before the year 2021. As if nothing changed.'

He was silent for a moment, scanning the looks of confusion on his students' faces, then restated, 'It's one of the curses of language, our own language which doesn't recognise the difference between a lion that grew up in the jungle and enjoyed all of its particularities, and a 'lion' that grew up in a prisoner in the circus, that spent its life as a clown.'

At that point, he bowed his head as if he sensed someone spying on him through an invisible keyhole. 'I fear we have become like that lion, caged by invisible wires, in a world we no longer recognise.'

In that moment, the wall-screens blinked off and the lights came back on. The teacher paused, and cast around at the young faces, suddenly aware that he had reached the end of the lesson. It was only a few moments before the wall-screens illuminated once more, announcing the commencement of the holiday. He forced a smile up at his students as they filed out.

'Happy Salvation Day to you and your loved ones.'

This was the moment Samir had been waiting for. He leapt up, unlocking the wheels in his shoes that propelled him outside before he had even thrown his red backpack over his shoulder. Helen watched him suspiciously before deciding to pack up her things and slip out after him.

Where in the world was that son of a bitch going?

More than anyone else, Helen knew how much he detested these 'soul-cleansing holidays,' as he used to call them. She skated along on the wheels of her shoes, descending three flights along the inclined bridges, finally turning right to find herself outside. She spotted him zipping between the hordes streaming along on their skates like a river that knew its way to the delta.

'Samir... Samir!' she shouted after him with all her might but without getting him to turn around, as he continued his descent.

'Samir... Samir!' She called out again but still he didn't respond, which only heightened her awkwardness, there in the street shouting his name. Here she was, for the thousandth time, reneging on her resolution to steer clear of this effortless charmer, her favourite classmate who filled her head with splendid, scorching thoughts: his translucent brownness, his hair tied up in a topknot that cascaded down again behind him. But in return, he also kept her at arm's length, being forever lost in his history books or trying to learn some ancient language, especially since he'd lost his mother the year before. From that day on, his behaviour had grown unpredictable. Once he appeared at a lecture dressed up like Gilgamesh, or 'Grandpa' as he called him, another time he turned up to a party in the guise of Husayn, another time Nebuchadnezzar, Moses and other strange characters nobody had heard of. His greatest obsession had become digging into the forgotten past of the city. Whenever she wanted to meet him it would be at one of those awful Pop Shop kiosks, that had first sprouted up when she was a kid, selling 'experience narratives', in tiny capsules. He would always take a few minutes to return to the street bench he was sat on, for his breathing to settle after the adventure he'd clearly been on.

She picked up her speed, zig-zagging between other, slower-moving pedestrians, and eventually managed to catch up with Samir. She whirled around in front of him, with arms out wide, to block his path.

Samir was so surprised that he would have crashed into her had she not swiftly side-stepped his unstoppable momentum, and caught his left hand between her fingers as he passed:

'Where are you off to now?' she whispered into his ear, as he came to a stop.

'I dunno.'

'I've been chasing you. When I ask you where you're going you won't even answer me. OK, so I've put on some weight. You haven't gone off me, have you?'

'Hala. Today's not your day.'

He kicked the back of his left heel and started moving again. But Helen still had hold of him. Eventually he turned to her, as they continued to glide in parallel, facing each other. 'OK, but not here,' he said, looking up at the date-vines that ran like a curtain around the buildings on both sides, each one embedded with synth-bio cameras.

Samir took Helen's hand and guided her off the Najaf Broadway, and down several side-streets until eventually they stopped outside a repeater station, where he knew there would be no trees to cause interference.

'Today is the day isn't it?' Helen asked when he was finally ready to talk.

'Take one of these and I'll tell you.' He held up a small blue pill in his left hand.

She stared at it.

'Pentathol,' she moaned. 'You don't trust me?'

'The Old City is my destiny, Hala. Come with me, then I will trust you.'

She snatched it out of his hand, and made it vanish leaving a smile on her face.

'By 'old city' you mean the 'Exhibition'?'

'Don't call it that, Hala. It is the real Najaf, not this wretched reboot; NJF.' He spat the letters out, like they had a sour taste.

'It's just a place for obsessives, Samir. It's unhealthy.'

'It's not up to me anymore.'

'Give me one reason why you have to go.'

He turned round, reluctantly, dropped his bag and lifted his shirt just above his belt. Helen saw it instantly and her eyes prickled.

The skin above his belt was cracking, a gap had opened up and started to peel, like an egg that had been slowly boiled.

'The symptoms!' she exclaimed.

'Yup.'

He fell silent and looked up to the sky which was being crisscrossed by lasers announcing the start of the holiday. He looked back at Helen.

'My father was one of the first doctors to study the disease; he identified many of its key stages, and risked his life in his research.'

'I know,' said Helen. 'I watched that blog-doc about him and how that first case, the swimmer who peeled to nothing in front of hundreds of spectators, had been his patient. That clip went viral at the time; it was sick.'

Helen shrugged. 'So,' she looked him straight in the eyes, 'you'll get the treatment... You'll be OK.'

'I don't want to. I want to follow it to the end, the way my mother did.'

'Your mum took her own life,' Helen said as softly as she could.

'No,' he said firmly, 'Something else happened. She knew it was leading somewhere, but when they took her dried-up body away from me, she was still there.'

'Samir. She's dead. That place is a cemetery, nothing more. People say it helps people mourn, but look at you, it's doing the opposite. It's twisted, Samir. You think she's still alive, just because her body is preserved. It's madness Samir!'

'My dad used his connections to return her to the Old City.'

'Samir...'

'Helen. There, there is no comma between life and death, down there. Everything is lifeless but alive.'

'So you go, and you find her; then what?'

'I might find a way of getting rid of this,' he said, pointing at his waist. 'And if I don't at least my last few days will be with her.'

'Does your father know what you're planning?'

'No,' he said, gesturing towards his backpack. 'It is better no one knows anything. I don't want to put them at risk.'

'Not even Aamir?'

'My brother?' he asked surprised. 'He'd be delighted to see the back of me; he's always been embarrassed by me, or scared my behaviour will affect his climb up the greasy pole.'

'Isn't he afraid for you?'

'Look, everything's prepared. I've had everything forged: my dad's fingerprints, his retinal scans... I've even impersonated his voice.' He lowered his pitch: 'My dearest Helen, take this ungrateful wretch away, and pray teach him some respect for his elders!'

Helen smiled.

'But you'll be found out, and then you'll get him into trouble too. They'll section you.'

'Maybe I am crazy. If so, let me just see her one last time; let me share my symptoms with her.'

'Don't leave me, Samir.'

At this, he said nothing, simply kissed her on the forehead. She turned away from him, resisting the urge to return the kiss. And so they stood together, not looking at each other in the silence, until suddenly the moment was broken by the sight of hundreds of people marching towards Celebration Square. Without looking back, Helen began to walk towards them, winding her way slowly through the crowd, who now streamed past her in the opposite direction, like some tidal wave.

It was too much. She made her way to the side of the street, and rested her back against the glass wall of the DNA Bank. Looking around, everything seemed distorted to her, like long jumbled sentences that had no meaning.

At that moment, it felt as if the city of NJF had transformed into a gigantic funfair, a carnival of technicolor billboards, skyscrapers cascading with light; each advertising message, scrolling across the sky in tortuous wordplay, promised a ride like no other, a once-in-a-lifetime 'experience narrative': Play or be Played.

Helen thought about her teacher's face and the circus lion, and the world suddenly struck her as not unlike like a child's toy grown monstrously large; it made her think, of how she and her friends would spend their weekends sitting in the stands of the Roman stadium, arms crossed, deciding collectively on the fate of particular players and their teams, at the start of each game; and how they would then imagine they were moving them around the pitch with their will power alone.

She sensed the building behind her shaking, and stepped forward a little in order to see its walls twisting, slowly but surely, above her, opening up to display its multi-level entrances. As some balconies closed in on themselves and others appeared, she recalled the advert a few weeks earlier: 'Lucky are those who live and work in the Transformer Buildings for they shall always enjoy a new view. Farewell solid walls!'

It was some spectacle.

It seemed human endeavour had now transcended the limitations of static architecture and buildings could dance like puppets.

Helen skated off again like someone late for a meeting, then, as if realising she'd missed it already, stopped suddenly, finding herself standing in front of a Pop Shop at the entrance to one of Najaf's busiest retail valleys. It was a deliberately retro version, aping the out-dated designs of the original kiosks, and staffed by an aquadroid – a laser hologram projected onto a cloud of smart-vapour.

'I'm exhausted, Bob,' Helen said, reading his name-tag. 'Give me your strongest.'

'How about a shot of High Gene?'

'No. Now's not the time for feeling happy,' she said, standing on one foot hesitantly. 'I want an anti-fear hormone. I feel like I'm living in a nightmare, and I just want to go back to sleep.'

'Something to impede the delivery from the adrenal gland?'

'Yes, *Anti-Fear.* That's the one. Make it a double.'

'Maybe you need some oxytocin, or some self-confidence hormone,' he suggested. 'Your eagerness to imbibe the aforementioned product, concerns me. Remember: reducing the distribution of adrenaline can be dangerous, and can lead to dependency. Why not try *Chillax* to help you relax?'

'Bob, please. I'm scared.'

'Of what?'

'I don't know. Maybe it's from the Transformer Buildings, or the light shows. Something's making me nervous, or rather unnerving me.'

'I'll give you Anti-Fear, madam, on the understanding that your use of it is prohibited for the next month. Your GP has just filed your dependency rating and you're low risk.' The aquadroid then handed her a shot glass, and changed its tone to deliver the usual product slogan. 'Life is but a dream...' It paused, leant in closer and whispered, 'so be careful waking up, Hala.'

Helen's blood ran cold. *Samir!* His name reverberated inside her. Samir was the only person who called her by that name, and hearing it again made her realize how she had prepared to never hear it again. She had abandoned him. And now she knew he was in danger. *They've discovered us Samir,* she thought to herself.

In an instant, Helen knew that all those compulsory implants, recording every detail of her blood chemistry since the day she was born, would today be registering something new, something rising within her. It wasn't fear, that old friend, but the *thing* she feared; and the sense that she would soon overcome it. She was standing now between two worlds; the one she had lived in all her life; and the one Samir was calling to her from: a strange place set back behind the walkways of ordinary life, extinct, forgotten, lifeless but alive. And to her, it seemed more attractive than anything this artificial world had to offer, this place where everything you touched became obsolete because you touched it, everything you said became a lie because you said it.

She looked hard and long at the shot glass in front of her.

What happened next she probably wouldn't be able to tell you. Samir's name rang through her thoughts, echoing, but with no reply. She was lost, calling his name, pleading, begging for forgiveness. Then suddenly a word. 'Come.' And with it a million unspoken co-ordinates, any one of which would lead her to him.

Within a matter of minutes she found herself running down a dark, narrow alleyway, one that seemed to be heading downwards, endlessly, completely at odds to the rest of the city's shape. Eventually she came to the end, and looked up at a huge iron gate, with only darkness behind it.

★

'What is this place?' Helen asked, staring at the massive columns of an enduring building, holding up a huge gold-coloured dome.

'It's a shrine,' Samir answered, taking her hand.

Helen tried to focus. Her stomach was still turning, the way it would if you'd just stepped out of an elevator that had plummeted a quarter of a mile in three seconds.

'A 'shrine'?'

'It's a kind of monument, attached to a grave in this case, designed to honour the memory of a hero, a prophet or a pious person.'

'And whose grave is this?'

'Imam `Ali,' said Samir. 'It is the centre around which this Old City was built.'

She had never heard of him, but she didn't ask any more questions, gazing up at the golden dome that looked like the helmet of some gigantic knight, bigger than her imagination could bear.

'Take your shoes off,' he said.

'Why?' Helen asked.

He stared at her as if searching for a convincing answer.

'We're here as guests, and we must follow the traditions of the hosts.'

She fought back a smile, recognising that Samir was trying on the role of scholar, despite the wonder in his eyes.

She started to circumambulate the grave, and on the far side spotted an old woman crouched near one corner, crying. Then she saw men, also with their hands held high.

'Was the suffering of our ancestors always so severe?' she asked, peering back between the mannequin-like figures.

He said nothing, but it didn't matter to Helen. She found herself entranced by the clothing these figures wore, astounded by its variety. She stopped beside a male statue who seemed to have been frozen just at the moment when his lips touched the golden mesh that surrounded the tomb.

'Were they worshipping the gold?' Helen asked. Samir again had no answer.

She walked away from him to watch one of those who had been praying – his hands spread open as if holding a book she couldn't see, his eyes gazing up imploringly towards the ceiling. She sidled up next to him, imitated his stance, and craned her neck to study his eyes; she couldn't find the strength to copy his upward stare, not with the same power or reverence.

'We've changed so much,' Samir mused, as if asking himself a question.

'The world changes and all we can do is try to keep up,' Helen offered.

'But have we changed for the *better*?' Samir asked.

Neither of them spoke.

'I like this place,' said Samir. But a doubt, like a microscopic crack, began to widen. 'Only…'

'Only what?'

'Nothing. Put your shoes on and let's get out of here.'

Beyond the temple, in the dim, yellow light shed by the organic halogens suspended high in the ceilings, the Old City revealed itself: a maze of crooked, narrow, streets, silted up with rubble, and decades' worth of moss and dark-coloured weeds. Under that high, oppressive ceiling – built over all effected cities in the years after 2021 – these streets felt smaller somehow, almost unimportant like the bookshelf aisles of an over-sized library. For that's what Old Najaf was now, a buried archive, a place where the past could be referenced, and drawn up into the conversations of the present, but only by academics on officially sanctioned research visits.

Even if there was enough light, the weeds and the rubble meant it was impossible for Helen or Samir to skate. The asphalt was either scratched and pockmarked with age, or ripped up decades ago by missile strikes, leaving huge craters. Helen walked on ahead excitedly, in awe of every new sight.

'What's that?' she cried out, pointing to a row of mysterious metal carcasses.

'They were called 'cars'.' Samir snorted. 'The dominant means of transit for over a century.'

'And what's happening there?'

She pointed to a group of figures wearing white robes, seated around a large cylindrical object, almost completely obscured with mould and weeds. Out of this bolus stretched a series of loose pipes, one to each of the men. Most of the figures held the ends of these pipes in their hands, but one seemed to have it leading straight into his mouth. Samir could not pretend to know what was happening here.

'But which of these were desiccated at the time of the outbreak, and which have been brought down here for storage?' Helen asked.

This one Samir could answer. 'All the recent victims of the syndrome are returned to domestic interior spaces, ideally ones shown to belong to ancestors or relatives of ancestors. The bodies out in the street are victims of the original outbreak'. At this Samir took the lead, picking up his pace and walking ahead of Helen, leading her along a route he knew off by heart. Eventually, they came to a large crater, which spanned the whole street and couldn't be circumnavigated. Having scrabbled first down and then up out of its tangle of weeds, they stood in front of a small, dilapidated house, that stood apart from the rest of the street. Samir's eyes blazed as he approached the front door.

As soon as Helen had crossed this tiny threshold, following close behind Samir, she could see, in the courtyard beyond, the macabre spectre of his mother waving directly back at them. Her carcass stood there, surrounded by a clutch of other relatives, presumably from several generations before, at the centre of a courtyard, built around a fountain where water had long stopped bubbling.

Samir fell silent immediately, tense with reverence, then proceeded to circle around the figure, slowly, muttering inaudible words as he did so. Helen held back, pretending to be more interested in the architecture of the house, in order to give him some privacy. Eventually she let herself glance out at Samir in the centre of the courtyard, and saw him leaning into the figure, very closely, as if trying to smell the carcass's hair. Helen couldn't look directly at the figure's face; its smile terrified her, regardless of the skin that surrounded it, cracked like the shell of a hardboiled egg, about to be peeled.

Seeing her look at him, Samir called back: 'Hala!' Then crossing the courtyard to where she stood, he took her hand and walked her back to figure.

'Mama. This is Hala, with whom I'm secretly in love.' Then Samir whispered something in Helen's ear that only the dead could hear.

Helen's cheeks flushed. She whispered back: 'I accepted you as a silent lover. Why wouldn't I accept you, loudly, as a husband?'

They both laughed and, on a sudden impulse, Helen kissed the statue's cheek before Samir pulled her back towards him. He wrapped his arms around her and planted a desperate kiss on her lips. Then he pulled her away from the statues, out of the courtyard altogether, and into a room at the front of the house, then up an ancient flight of stairs.

It was difficult for Helen to understand what was happening. In that moment, Samir's breath became like a voice in a dream; an echo with no body attached, for neither of them had bodies, here, not bodies as they had been, separate, discrete, disloyal. As Samir tore off Helen's clothes she didn't feel as though she were undressing in a graveyard city, or a place that had been abandoned by the living since 2017, 86 years before.

In the bedroom Helen discovered that Samir was a virgin; she had guessed as much from his behaviour at college, but now it was confirmed by his nervousness. She wanted to engulf him. She wanted to plunge his face into her bare chest, as if to nurse him, and as her lust soared she threw him down on the bed and started to bite at his chest. As he entered her, his fevered kisses grew more rapid, spread out over her face and temples, gently at first and then with greater and greater savagery, pushing her to the point where she cried at the top of her voice, as if to make herself heard out in the courtyard.

*

Helen stirred and was alarmed to find herself completely naked under the blanket, alongside Samir. She wriggled free from his arm, propped her head up, and looked at him.

'I wonder what our teacher would say if we brought him here?'

'Mr. Farhan?'

'Yeah, I never saw him more emotional than the time he talked about those two lions – the one in the jungle and the one in the circus.'

'Poor man, he was just nostalgic for this dead world...'

A rustle came from outside the room, like someone

walking towards them. Helen raised her finger to Samir's lips before he could say anything.

'Can you hear it?' she whispered.

'What is it?'

'It sounds like someone eating,' she replied hesitantly.

'There's someone *else* down here!?'

They listened until chewing became crunching: a drier, scratchier sound that grew closer and closer. Samir got up and tiptoed to the door, unashamed in his nakedness. Helen also got up but made for the closet at the side of the room instead, and beckoned him over.

'Sshhh,' she whispered as he had climbed gently in beside her.

They stood there in the darkness listening to the sound of someone eating, almost imperceptible at first, but gradually it grew louder and louder. Samir held the closet door to, but his hand was shaking. Whatever it was it was definitely getting closer, though neither of them could see anything through the slats in the closet door. Samir seemed to be holding his breath indefinitely; his shaking was getting worse. Helen feared it would soon make the whole closet rattle. All of sudden, Samir exploded, bursting out of the closet, and throwing the door to the room open. As he did so, however, he let out a wild, uncontrolled yelp, and leapt high in the air. Something dashed across the floor, into the room, making straight for the closet, which Helen vacated almost as quickly as Samir had.

A rat! Helen threw herself onto Samir and they both fell on the bed laughing.

'Dear God!' Samir laughed. 'Among all this death – only the rats survived!'

Helen replied with more kisses, and Samir threw a shoe at the closet. The creature promptly scuttled out, made its way along the wall, and eventually, after another shoe was thrown, left the room forever.

'What did that fucker want in the there anyway?' Samir asked, but it was Helen who got to her feet, and walked back to the closet.

She leant inside and felt something hanging in there.

'Look what I found!' she said, returning to the bed, holding a long, white, perfectly smooth robe.

'A dishdasha!' Samir exclaimed.

Helen removed the hanger and as Samir got to his feet, held it against him.

'It's your size!'

'Nah!' said Samir, smiling.

'Please!' Helen begged. 'I'd love to see you wearing one of these!'

'Why?'

'Because you want to be one of them, don't you? You always have.'

'Not after today, seeing all this,' Samir gestured at the museum-world outside.

'Imagine, wearing it up there, back in class!'

Samir smiled and reached for her hand. 'I'll take it back with us. But not to wear, OK?'

Najufa

Ibrahim al-Marashi

AT THE PASSPORT CONTROL of Baghdad International Airhub, I scanned my index finger in front of the droid, but the mock Ishtar Gate of alternating blue and yellow Teflon bricks failed to slide open.

'Muhammad, your Iraqi passport is embedded in your *middle* finger,' my grandfather, Isa, reminded me.

'Thank you, Jidu.'[1]

We were travelling with a 72-strong hamla[2], a pilgrimage organised by the Iraqi Shi'a community of Alaska, and were lucky to be the first of them to enter baggage claim. On collecting our aircases, we were met by our assigned droids, Abbas R-12 and Zaynab C-12, our guides in Iraq.

While waiting for the others, I double-tapped my forehead to call up the local weather report, even though we'd barely be stepping outdoors. It was 52 degrees in Baghdad, a cool January day for that city. I couldn't help check the weather back in Alaska too. 35 degrees. There must have been a warm breeze blowing in from the South Canadian deserts that morning.

'Have you called your father to let him know you've arrived safely?'

'I don't have to, Jidu. Your status automatically updates when you land.'

'It would be nice for him to hear your voice, at least.'

'I'll call him when we get to Najufa.'

Once all 72 members of our hamla had gathered in front

of the droids, Abbas instructed us, in Iraqlish, to follow the two of them to the station where we'd take the maglev direct to Najufa. Before we'd even started walking, however, Umm Hayder, seeing something to her right, suddenly stopped: 'Yaaa. Duty Free!', and snapping her fingers at Abbas, 'Ya hajji droid! Khalina fed daqiqa[3] so we can buy fed shii.'[4]

For a moment, the red LED-pupils in Abbas's eyes looked furious. Droids hate being called 'droids'. Each one has an official job title, and if the AI Revolution in China had taught us anything, it was that they deserved respect for their work. Abbas' title was 'Automated Liaison to the Holy Sites'. But old prejudices are hard to kick, especially around people of senior years.

Abbas said, 'No. Maku waqt[5] for shopping. We will miss the...'

But before he could finish his sentence, Umm Hayder and her seven kids had abandoned their aircases and fled to the Duty Free zone, with others following close behind.

Abbas stood next to me, tilting his head in disapproval. 'I cannot condone this disregard for the schedule, this... shqad hosa!'[6]

My grandfather whispered, 'Look at the other hamlas. So organised.'

A guide-droid spoke in Urdulishto to an orderly group of Pakistani Shi'as stood nearby, while a party of East African Shi'as walked in unison towards the station, led by a droid draped in an elegant, orange thobe.

Abbas R-12 and Zaynab C-12 finally returned from Duty Free, herding back the strays to our hamla, and we arrived at our platform just as the train was about to close its doors. Fifteen minutes later, the train made its first stop at Karbalafor where more pilgrims climbed aboard.

As the train waited, I told my chair to move to the upright position, shifting from 'vigorous' to 'gentle' massage. 'Jidu, how long did it take your father to get from Baghdad to Najufa on his ziyarat?'[7]

'It was just "Najaf" back then.'

'Of course.' My history was terrible. After 2003, Najaf, I knew, had grown rapidly and eventually merged completely with the nearby city, Kufa.

'So, do you want to know about his first trip in 1979, or his last in 2010?'

'1979. The first.'

'He would have only been five at the time. I think he said it took about three hours, but many of his "memories" from the trip were taken from what his mom told him later. They stopped at the Nus-khana, a rest-stop café, on the way, I know that. He talked about his parents making him a sandwich out of two English tea-biscuits, with a piece of lokum in between. It's strange the details she recounted. He described it to me as like a s'more, but with Turkish Delight instead of marshmallow in the middle.'

'That was so like my grandmother, always feeding everyone halwiyat.[8] My father probably had cavities in his milk teeth!'

'And in 2010?'

'That trip took them over seven hours. Seven long hours with my father, in his late 30s, crammed in beside *his* father, on what they called an 'omnibus' – a kind of large car, with many wheels. It took them that long because every thirty minutes they had to stop at another checkpoint. The takfiris always targeted those checkpoints with car bombs, as there were always police there. Each time my father's omnibus stopped, he would stare out of the window at the car in the next lane, thinking: *This is the car that will explode next.*'

I glanced out of the window as the last pilgrims boarded. It made sense to build a maglev connecting Baghdad to the shrine cities. Building the entire system underground must have been for security reasons.

'My father agreed to make that second trip, in 2010, simply to accompany his by-then aging parents, fearing for their safety. They had insisted on going that year, even though it was still dangerous, because they were convinced the US was about to re-instate some kind of neo-Ba'athist government, in a last ditch attempt to restore some kind of order. The more my father mocked this conspiracy theory, the more they stuck to it.'

The maglev started again.

'Why were your grandparents so scared of the Ba'ath?'

'My grandparents, Morteza and Biba, never lived in Iraq while Saddam was President. That was close to 20 years. They were scared they might be thrown in jail if they went back. Just having lived in the US was enough for the mukhabarat to accuse you of being a spy.'

'Oh. You mean the *old* mukhabarat.'

I remembered from my history-casts that 'mukhabarat' once meant Saddam Hussein's ubiquitous secret police – very different from the current 'mukhabarat', 'The Directorate of Public Security Droids', which were introduced to smoke out the remaining sleeper cells of ISJISL, the Islamic State of Jordan, Iraq, Syria, and Lebanon in the late 2080s.

Jidu never told me why he, personally, never visited Iraq. Isa's father, Ibrahim, had never wanted to take them there. I knew that they had all grown up in Baltimore, while wars were raging in Iraq, making any visit impossible, and then when they moved to Alaska, and it declared independence, visas to the oil zones were nigh-on impossible. But he could have visited more recently. We all suspected he was slightly scared of it. His bedtime podcasts to us, as kids, had all been uttered in hushed and reverent tones, even when describing Najaf during the hard times. But they were all made up of other peoples' scattered memories. He had never been. I had decided to finally drag him there, hoping he would realise he had nothing to fear; new experiences of the place could integrate with old, handed-down legends. The two weren't mutually exclusive. Jidu always said that the second trip, in 2010, had transformed his father, Isa's life, and stood as a turning point for the whole family. None of them ever went back.

Fortunately our ten-star hotel was connected to the station by an air-conditioned moving walkway. It seemed from the many other pilgrims being conveyed towards it, that only Alaskan-Iraqis were staying at this hotel, and naturally all of them were doctors. It was 8:30pm and 51 degrees outside.

'I wish this thing moved faster,' I complained.

'You know, in 2010 all motorised conveyances were banned in Najaf,' Jidu began. 'Those takfiris were targeting crowded markets with their car-bombs. So cars were not allowed into town. Imagine travelling for hours on an omnibus, like my father, only to then be dropped off on the outskirts of the town. "Thank Allah," my father would say, "for the young boys with their horses and wooden carts appearing from nowhere to carry all their luggage, and some of the older people too." Can you imagine walking alongside an animal!'

'Zayn. Aftahamat. I get it. I'll stop complaining.'

Once up in our rooms, I deactivated my aircase and watched it hover gently to the ground. 'Call Dr. Allawi', I said. It had been difficult to find someone to take on my scheduled neural-chip interface surgeries at the hospital, and I wanted to see how my wife was getting on with the extra workload. She didn't pick up.

'Did you call your father?'

'Yes... I will... just let me relax for a minute.'

In an attempt to distract Jidu, I moved to the window and pointed below. 'Look. We have a perfect view of the hadhra!' I tap-activated my telescopic retina, and scanned the shrine's golden dome and four minarets, illuminated by the floodlights.

'What is that smaller hadhra next to Imam Ali's?'

Jidu paused. 'My father never mentioned a second hadhra.' Then he clicked his fingers. 'Aha. That must be the shrine of Sayyid Ali Sistani. Sistani in the 2020s finally got

Iraqis to stop killing each other. When he eventually passed away in the 50s, all the Shi'as, Sunnis, Christians, and Sushis poured into the streets equally to mourn him.'

Again I struggled to remember my history-casts. The Sushis – children of intermarried Sunnis and Shi'as – had formed their own militia in the early 20s, and had pushed back the takfiris from the cities into the deserts. That was when they were just called 'ISIS', but in the deserts they regrouped and redirected their mania towards Jordan and Lebanon, becoming ISJISL. It was hard to imagine that these crazies were once even more feared, as a terrorist group, than CAKA, the Christian Assembly of Kansas and Arkansas.

I stared at the jagged skyline in front of us.

'My father described this city as a ghost-town in 2010.'

'That was almost a century ago, now Jidu.' When Iraq's oil fields ran dry in 2050, pilgrimage traffic became Iraq's greatest revenue generator, making the cities of Najufa, Karbala, and Kadhimayn the nation's wealthiest.

'Ani so *ta'aban*', I said, and then commanded my bed to remove the blankets and sheets. I dropped down on the edge of it and unzipped the foot-soles from my one-suit. 'I think I will take my vapour shower in the morning, before we go to the hadhra.'

'If *you're* tired, imagine how *they* felt,' he began, launching into yet another set of comparisons. I had half-expected him to be morose when we got here, disappointed by things looking so different from how he'd pictured them. I thought *I* would be the one to do the all the talking. No such luck.

'Are you jaw'an?'

'No jidu. I took a dinner pill at the airport,' I replied, lying face down on the bed.

'Zayn. How about we go to the lobby for some chay.'

'Chay!' I sat up. 'You know you can't drink it.'

'I know, but I just want you to try your first glass of real Iraqi tea.'

'Khosh. I'll have a chay-droid bring some up to the room,' I said, looking for the room service button.

'No. I want you to have it in the lobby.'

I looked across at him.

'Please. To make your jidu happy. So we can have a moment together, create a new memory.'

'OK, OK.'

Taking my first sip, I said, 'Jidu, I wish you could enjoy it with me.'

'May khalif. The chay you are drinking will never be like the chay they had back then. In the 20th and early 21st century, Iraqis used to make it from a samawar with half a cup of tea and half a cup of sugar resting on the bottom.'

'Samawar shinnu?' I asked, blowing on my tea to cool it down.

'That was a contraption where boiling water underneath percolated upwards through the tea leaves in a chamber at the top. Nowadays the samawar is no doubt somewhere inside the chay-droid; obviously you can't see it. And the leaves are synthetic now, of course.'

'I can't imagine what tea with real sugar tastes like. Too much, I suspect.' The Great Global Drought happened just before I was born. After that, the Glucose Cartels became sole share holders in the few remaining sugarcane fields, and possession of un-rationed glucose was upgraded to the same criminality rating as possession of synth-narcotics.

My grandfather stopped talking, having finally acknowledged the others filling up the lobby – families with kids running around, pilgrims returning from their final evening prayers.

'All my grandfather wanted, it seems, was to sit around Najaf in hotel lobbies, drinking tea. My father accompanied him, reluctantly, nervously eying everyone around them, suspecting every pilgrim, and every member of the hotel staff of being a takfiri. After 2003, my great-uncle, who was living in Baghdad at the time, was kidnapped because he was known to be well off. When the ransom demand came, his family tried to barter over the price, you know, because that's what Iraqis do. Haggle.'

'That's why your grandmother told you all never to say you were from America,' I said, waving the chay-droid over for a refill.

'Of course'. The minute the chay-droid had finished pouring, Jidu asked it if it was from Najaf. When the droid said, 'yes', Jidu added, 'My great-grandfather, Hassan, was from Najaf.' He then launched into a retelling of a large swathe of the paternal family history: recounting the details of Hassan's flight from Najaf in the 1920s, being imprisoned by the British, discovering one of the prison guards was Hassan's former neighbour, escaping prison with his help, fleeing to Iran, and eventually taking a ship to Zanzibar. The waiter stood there and smiled, knowing the protocol for listening to older guests. Jidu regaled him with the finer points of Hassan's son, Morteza's journey to Baghdad in the fifties, to study medicine, how he then moved to London, became a British citizen, went back to Baghdad to marry, and then moved to Maryland, to practice neurology at John Hopkins University. Jidu was lucky it *wasn't* 2010. He may as have been screaming to the entire lobby, *I am a wealthy North American. Kidnap me!*

I yawned in between sips from the second cup.

'OK. You're tired. We can go back upstairs.' He had merely wanted to see me relax in a hotel lobby without the fear his father had, and which I suspect he had too. 'No. I am listening. Keep talking.'

'Get your rest. We will have to do a lot of walking tomorrow. And out in the heat too.'

I assumed I would have no problem sleeping. I took a blast of water vapour from the nightstand and thought about calling my wife. Maybe even Dad. I got up and walked towards the window. It was 3am and the floodlights were still illuminating the shrine.

'You can't sleep?' Jidu chuckled.

I waited in the darkness for his next line. For a moment it didn't seem to come.

'My father couldn't sleep on his first night in Najaf.'

'There it is.'

'There what is? Anyway, my father had food poisoning from a kebab he'd eaten and it kept him up all night vomiting. Biba had to sit beside him all night – a man in his late 30s, reduced to a crumpled mess on the bathroom floor, needing his mother.

'So he went to Najaf to connect to his Iraqi roots, and all he came back with were some Iraqi viruses.'

'Funny.'

'He went to Iraq to look after his parents. But his mom ended up looking after him.'

Jidu fell silent.

'So she gave him Prilosec for the stomach acid in his throat?'

'Very impressive. They taught you early 21st century drugs in medical school then. Yes, Biba famously kept a stash of every medicine known to man in her handbag, at all times. And that night, Biba and Morteza argued into the small hours about what medicine they should give poor Ibrahim. It's convenient having one parent as a doctor, my father used to say, but a disaster having two.'

I stared at the ceiling. 'How do you know all this, in such detail, Jidu? It wasn't you that made these trips!'

'I've told you. The casts my father, Ibrahim, recorded, before he got ill. He made dozens of them back in the 70s, when he had this mad scheme to publish a Bio-blog. I found them a few years ago and got a friend to convert them all to optic files. I listened to them all the time now. Here,' he sat up suddenly. 'Let me play you the bit about the night he was sick.' He tapped his forehead three times, and mumbled a series of prompt words, like quiet grunts to himself: 'Archive', 'Ibrahim', 'Najaf', '2010', 'Keyword "plastic gun"', 'Play paragraph'.

Suddenly the air in the room was alive, crackling with the strange, amplified background noises and a voice so formal it was like being at mosque.

'It was barely three in the morning,' the voice croaked. 'I had returned to bed, and lay there listening to mother and father arguing, staring out the window. The entire facade of the hotel seemed to be made out of glass, you understand, and my bed was right up against it; the whole wall as a window. So I was lying on my side, watching the nocturnal world below. We were only on the third floor, and I could clearly see a policeman standing at a checkpoint, holding something in his hand. It was an odd looking device – like a plastic gun with a silver antenna coming out the top. I presumed it was for detecting car-bombs. It scanned for a kind of wiring apparently only used in explosive devices. I must have seen other detectors before, but as I lay there I couldn't stop staring at the contraption, and wondering what the procedure was exactly, if the light on the top flashed on. Shoot to kill instantly, I presume. Hope it wasn't a faulty reading.'

The call to prayer could be clearly heard, starting up in the background.

'There was no traffic, of course,' the voice continued. 'And only official vehicles were allowed that far into town. But he still stood there, like a statue, pointing that machine down an empty street. I later learned those devices never actually worked. Some British guy made millions selling the Iraqi government those things, and they became standard issue at every checkpoint. It later turned out he had just repurposed a metal detector mechanism, set to never pick up anything.'

'How things have changed,' Jidu said, double-tapping his head to pause the tape, before muttering, 'Play.'

'After the introduction of military droids in the mid 20s, the Iraqi government brought in an army of robots to replace policemen at checkpoints. Their sensors were actually able to detect things this time – semtex, nitroglycerene, napalm – and at a distance of half a kilometre. Car-bombs became a thing of the past. And so did the culture of fear and suspicion. During the Sectarian Wars, police at the checkpoints had asked to see every driver's ID, and from their last name, they could tell if they were Shi'a or Sunni. If you were Sunni, you weren't allowed to enter. Shi'a areas began to develop their own autonomy, like Muhafazat al-Sadr, which grew out of what was once 'Sadr City', a sprawling Baghdad slum; they became independent provinces, connected by a network of Shi'a-only tunnels. In the darkest days of the Wars, you could be killed at a checkpoint any day of the week, just for belonging to the wrong sect. The droids, by contrast, were like guardian angels. They were only interested in detectable chemicals, not family histories or possible allegiances. Droids didn't ask you for an ID card. Suddenly, the Iraqi people felt free again.

'Anyway, I was lying in my bed, staring at this policeman, for what must have been hours. I was imagining what would happen if a car were to appear at the end of that empty road, speeding towards us, and if the policeman wasn't a good shot. The explosion would shatter the glass of this wall-high window and obliterate the three of us. I had a very strong sense, all of a sudden, of what it would be like to bleed to death, dismembered. Different parts of myself, in different parts of the room.'

Jidu and I lay there in the dark. The background noises continued, but the voice had paused. It occurred to me that pilgrimages were supposed to be journeys of the spirit, but for Jidu, this was a journey of the macabre, a rendezvous with ghosts. Was this the turning point in my great-grandfather's life?

I commanded the blankets to cover me again and resolved to sleep. But Jidu wasn't finished.

'There's something about that phrase,' Jidu said, clearly to himself now, 'that haunts me: "different parts of myself". '

'Go to sleep, Jidu,' I grunted. 'Go to sleep.'

The following morning we were back down in the lobby, asking the breakfast-droids for top-ups of coffee vapour, breathing them in with slow, satisfied delight. 'Ah, that's better,' my grandfather sighed – his first fully formed sentence of the day. He then muttered something to the droid who returned with a bowl of what looked like white cream. 'Now, this is gaymer,' Jidu said, excitedly. 'Originally gaymer was made from fresh goat's milk, mixed with a form of glucose made by insects – *by insects can you believe!* They called it "honey". And then there was the bread, the samun – delivered fresh from the baker that morning, made from wheat fresh from the fields that summer.'

I tried a spoonful of the substance, and responded with my mouth still full: 'I know, I know, nothing is how it was in your day.'

Jidu paused for a moment and then asked, 'Did you call your father to let him know you arrived?'

We ate in silence. Half an hour later, Abbas R-12 and Zaynab C-12 entered the lobby and informed us that we were to finish our breakfast quickly as the shrine of Imam Ali tour was about to leave.

As we stepped out into the heat, we tried to imagine how hot it would be if the street-level air-conditioning wasn't working. As the walkway conveyed us toward the shrine, vendors stepped on and off, trying to sell us anything from hovering prayer rugs and turquoise Teflon jewellery, to bootleg neural implants. None of us could be tempted and each of the vendors politely stepped off, before their allotted two minutes had elapsed. The shrine of Imam Ali was now in front of us. At the landing platform, a large crowd had gathered already, and our guide droids had to snake a path through it for us to follow. As we walked, I tapped my forehead: 'Reference: What is Najufa's current population?' The implant search-engine pulled up the result. 'Three million, five hundred and seventy two thousand, eight hundred and thirty four, excluding visitors.' Thousands of visitors added to this, of course, arriving by train from Baghdad and Tehran every day.

'Najaf was only half a million in 2003,' my grandfather chipped in.

After giving me his estimate on what proportion of the local population was made up of people on temporary contracts, and therefore 'not permanent,' he fell silent again. He must have been slightly overwhelmed by the range of languages being spoken around him as we walked the avenue leading into the shrine. In his day there was standard Arabic, or fusha, and the Iraqi amiyah or dialect, which differed slightly from city to city. But here there was a cacophony of dialect amalgams: Sorani-Dari, Franco-Farsi, Kumanji-Turkmen. People seemed thoroughly promiscuous with what they chose to mix with what.

As we entered into the shrine, three election-droids approached us, noting our accents. Since Iraqis in the diaspora could now vote in national elections, we had been targeted for slogans and manifesto promises on behalf of the State of Technology Coalition Party.

'There was something called an 'election' the year my father came here,' Jidu started up again, somewhat inevitably. 'In those days, the politicians were merely tribal leaders, religious figures, or militiamen wanting to widen their power. Ordinary, decent people attempted to form a coalition, but their innocence was the reason they lost.'

'But modern elections are just as corrupt,' I suggested, as we approached the shrine's sahn.[9] Today's human politicians never set foot among ordinary people to deliver their message, and the most successful parties were simply those that struck the sweetest deals with the search-engine corps. In Jidu's father's time, people had voted for a party's political or religious program. Now all that counted was its digital affiliations. All of them claimed to represent both man and mechanoid equally, but in reality it was still a small number of exclusively human shareholders that were striking the search-engine deals, behind closed doors.

As our hamla filed into the sahn, the women split off towards their section, led by Zaynab, while we followed Abbas. Two guard droids stood at the door, scanning us closely to see if anyone's body language triggered their 'threat' algorithms; excessive sweating, shaking, twitching, vocal tension, and so on. Eight years ago, a sleeper *takfiri,* had posted an encrypted 'allegiance blog' to the long dormant ISJISL, before kidnapping a chay-droid and hacking it. Packed with explosives, all undetectable beneath a lead-lined chasis, the chay-droid had approached a popular mosque in Karbalafor. It could not have known that the garbage collectors in the street outside were actually undercover mukhabarat-droids. Detecting a closed safety-loop in its command code, the mukhabarat fired a Tau beam into its legs, disabling it. To make an example of it, to *other* droids, it was put on trial, found guilty, and disassembled slowly, in full power mode, live on public access holo-TV.

Since then, people have been nervous about making pilgrimages. Some package tours even included a 'Quick Will' service, just in case.

'It is so strange to just enter the hadhra like this,' I said, as we simply walked through the courtyard towards the ablutions fountain.

'Why is it strange?' Jidu replied.

As we reached the fountain, a wudhu-droid approached me. I unzipped the arms and feet of my one-suit, and stood in front of him as he sprinkled salty water vapour into my hands. It must have been desalinated, piped in from the Gulf via the Fourth and Fifth Canals, as it was completely odourless. I washed both sides of my face, and then my arms, and feet. I was ready to pray.

'It looks exactly the same,' my jidu was saying. 'Exactly how it was in all those photos!'

He was kind of right. The actual shrine covering Imam Ali's body probably hadn't changed. But the complex itself had undergone numerous expansions to accommodate the growth in pilgrims.

I doubled-tapped to zoom my retinas, so that I could scan the whole complex: the crystal chandeliers, the high glass walls, the blue crystal tiles, reflecting the sky, the jade marble archways, and finally the great cube-like structure encasing Imam Ali's body itself, with its latticework of silver and gold. It was surrounded by a throng of pilgrims, and I, like everyone else, pushed forward to touch it.

'Careful Muhammad. Don't push others. Be patient. Don't be like my father when he first saw this shrine.'

I grabbed the silver mesh with my right hand, and with my left beckoned my grandfather toward me to touch it also. All the time, he whispered a prayer. There were so many pilgrims trying to touch the shrine that we could barely stand there a minute before the guard-droids moved us on.

We found an empty space a few metres away and sat down on the carpeted floor, looking back at the shrine and the pilgrims gathering around it.

'You know, my father had memories of seeing this shrine when he was just five years old. All that crystal, it stuck with him. He told me he had a Lone Ranger mask in his pocket. It was what he called a 'cowboy' – some kind of mythical hero-character from two centuries back. This character used to wear a black mask just around his eyes. My father, casually put this mask on, only to be screamed at by his mother: "You can't be the Lone Ranger in the hadhra!"'

We both smiled. 'When they came again in 2010, my father and grandfather sat down – who knows, maybe even on this very spot,' Jidu continued. 'But within minutes of them getting comfortable my grandfather suddenly jumped up again: "We should go and find your mum!" My father protested, "Baba! We just got here. Can't we just enjoy this?" But my grandfather had barely been separated from Bibi for five minutes, and he needed to be with her again. They were in the presence of their revered Imam Ali, who they hadn't seen since 1979, and all his grandfather could think about was getting back to Bibi. It wasn't enough to be there with his only son. So they packed up and went looking for her. She was still in the women's section, and they had to wait at the entrance for her, for more than an hour before she emerged. And that was it. Then they left.'

'I don't get it.' I finally broke. 'I don't get it, Jidu. What was so important about this trip? Why have you spent years obsessing over it? This trip that was *their* story, not yours?'

Hearing the tone of my voice, three guard-droids and a muezzin-droid simultaneously stopped in their tracks and turned towards us.

'I'm getting to it, Muhammed. Even those five minutes sitting in the presence of the shrine was enough to change my father's life. Sitting in front of Imam Ali's body, he realised this wasn't just a Shi'a place, this wasn't even just a muslim place, this was a place special to all people, of all religions, and those without religion too. This was a place for reconnecting. That's what Baba hated so much about the 2003 War, and the Sectarian Wars that followed. Before 2003, he never thought about which of his muslim friends were Sunni and which Shi'a. It occurred to him, afterwards, that most of them had actually been Sunnis, before the invasion. But after 2003, he could think of nothing else. Baba's uncle was kidnapped and killed in 2007, igniting a hatred that was already roaring within him by then. For three further years, it raged in him, darkening his eyes. He used to say to me, 'In my heart. I was as bad as them.' But then in 2010, just five minutes of sitting here made him realise there are no Sunnis and Shi'as, just brothers and sisters – this wasn't just a Shia place, but the resting place of a great common ancestor, the Imam Ali. That's why we're called 'sayyids', Muhammed. We can trace our descent to him. And at that moment, sitting here, Baba thought to himself: "What would Ali, our ancestor think of the person I have become, so consumed by hate and vengeance. What would he think of me judging an entire people based on what a few criminals have done?" And just as his father was fussing over finding Bibi, *my* father, Ibrahim, was suddenly feeling all his hate being released.'

He saw I was looking down, and paused.

'My father said that being here made him think of his other ancestors. When he touched that silver mesh in 2010, he knew he was touching something that his father, and his father's father had touched many times themselves. Something, for instance, that his great-grandfather Hassan must have touched in 1920, before fleeing the city with his family, having fought in the Great Revolt that year against the British. And when Hassan tried to make his way back from Zanzibar in 1960, via mainland Africa, he got as far as Arusha, in Tanzania, and was buried in the foothills of Kilimanjaro. He died before my father was born, of course.'

'What I can't understand,' I began cautiously, 'is why you never came here before? You talked about this pilgrimage of your father's for years, but you never came here yourself.'

Jidu was quiet. 'I went on another pilgrimage once,' he began eventually. 'I went with my father, Ibrahim, in the 70s, after Mum died. We went to Zanzibar. To stand on the island in the hope that he could reconnect with the landscape of his father's childhood. That was the plan, at least. But nothing looked the same as the old photos. It was just desert by then. But while we were there, we managed to hop over to Arusha to visit his grandfather Hassan's grave.'

'You never told me this, Jidu.'

'That was my greatest pilgrimage, Muhammad. Until today.'

I smiled up at him.

'And my father was almost as annoying as you to travel with!' he laughed.

'So you have a great-great-grandfather buried under a mountain in Africa? And your great-grandfather?'

'Beside a freeway in northern California.'

'I wish I could have met them both. But why did you never come *here*?'

'I'm trying to tell you. You see, in my own troubles with my father, I idolised his predecessors instead, people like Hassan. I think you are doing the same with me... Don't be angry with your father for wishing to end my life. Seeing me transition to a singularity has been hard for him. Knowing, I'm first part-machine and then, soon, will be all-machine troubles him, more than it does me.' Jidu's blue eyes glinted in the sunlight. 'Who'd have thought he would turn out to be the old-fashioned one, not me? I was happy to go quietly into the organic night as well, but then you came along.'

'Why are you telling me this?'

'Because it has happened already, my child. All of it. I haven't been honest with you. The transition is complete. We haven't talked about it, but you know it to be true. I'm now just a hologram; just a network of algorithms responding to stimuli and playing out scenarios. Recorded by an implant I carried round in me for years, and then transferred to an implant in *you*, Muhammed, so I could accompany you on this trip.'

I stared at him.

'They said you would struggle with this part.'

'What part?' I blurted out. I was shaking, but the security droids had long since moved along.

'I want you to do this here.'

'I can't,' I said, looking at him through tears, knowing instantly what he meant.

'All of my ancestors were connected to Najaf but none of them were buried there. I ask you now to rectify that, to do me one last favour. Let me have my final moment here.'

'Don't you want to see your great-grandchildren?'

'Of course I do. But it will be too painful not to hold them. This is not me, Muhammed. I am not me... I know that now. Bring your children here, and your grandchildren. Let them see this place that has survived so many centuries of hardship. Let them see the place where you made the hardest decision of your life.'

I sat there. I don't know for how long. My jidu was silent.

'Ok. This is it. Allah wiyak, Jidu.'

'Thank you, my boy.'

I opened the panel on my sleeve. Among language implants, phone chips and neural website routers, I ejected my grandfather's card and held it in the open air. I dropped my head and let my hands do what they needed to, knowing that nearly a century's worth of memories were being obliterated, letting the pieces fall to the carpet.

I left the shrine without telling Abbas and ducked into the first jewellery stall I saw, to buy a cheap necklace made of bright blue Teflon. *Who is this for?* I thought to myself, and started laughing. Then, when the giggles had passed, I stepped outside, and tapped my forehead: 'Call Dad.'

Notes

1. jidu: 'grandfather'.
2. hamla: 'delegation'.
3. fed daqiqa: 'just a minute'.
4. fed shii: 'something'.
5. maku waqt: 'no time'.
6. shqad hosa: 'what a mess'.
7. ziyarat: 'visits'.
8. halwiyat: 'sweets'.
9 sahn: 'courtyard'.

Afterword

THE BEST SCIENCE FICTION, they say, tells us more about the context it's written in than the future it's trying to predict. The future may offer a blank canvas onto which writers can project their concerns, in new and abstract ways, but the concerns themselves are still very much 'of their time'.

This was the thinking behind *Iraq + 100*: to offer writers a space in which to explore the troubles of the present, many of which were direct consequences of the 2003 invasion, in an uninhibited way – through the allegory of the future, or through the long lens of speculative fiction. It was also an invitation to construct *positive* visions of Iraq's future, stories of hope and speculations on what long-term peace and self-determination might look like.

When Hassan and I first devised the commission, in late 2013, the tenth anniversary of the invasion of Iraq had just passed. We both found ourselves wondering if the horror and scale of that atrocity would now, in Britain at least, be neatly packed away and sent down into the long, high-vaulted archive of 'crimes this country has committed abroad', never to trouble the British conscience again. We wanted to commission a book that kept the consequences of 2003 at the forefront of reader's minds; one that presented them anew, somehow – even if that meant dressing them up in the shiny future-dress of science fiction. We also wanted to invite other Iraqi writers into the space that had been created by Hassan's own literary success,[1] as suddenly, there was a genuine appetite for new fiction from Iraq.

A call for submissions was posted in late 2013, and stories started coming in from all over the world – both from writers inside Iraq, and Iraqi diaspora writers elsewhere in the world – many of them showing a flare for the surreal and the fantastical that Hassan's readers will recognise. (Three of the stories here, being written in English, were selected by myself, rather than Hassan, so in that regard the editorial duties were shared.)

Then, in June 2014, everything changed. Mosul fell to IS, and a new war spread its shadow across the country. The long-term consequences of the 2003 invasion were suddenly, tragically, back at the forefront of people's minds. No one needed any reminders. On top of this, the very existence of Iraq, as a distinct sovereign entity, had become uncertain.

Many of the stories gathered in this book were written *before* this second invasion, and some readers may feel this automatically puts them out of step with events unfolding on the ground; the immediate reality of Iraq has since become more terrifying and unpredictable than anything fiction could envision, even for the distant future. But Hassan and I stand by all of these stories – whether written before or after June 2014 – for they offer glimpses at a genuinely different Iraq; one in which the original ambitions of the country's capital, founded by Caliph al-Mansur as the 'City of Peace', might still be detected; one in which the great scientific aspirations of that Round City, and its House of Wisdom,[2] might one day be realised.

Ra Page, October 2016

Notes

1. Hassan Blasim's *The Iraqi Christ* won the 2014 Independent Foreign Fiction Prize and his two collections have now been published in 23 different languages.
2. C.f. Hassan's Foreword.

About the Authors

Hassan Abdulrrazak is an author of Iraqi origin, born in Prague and living in London. His plays include *Baghdad Wedding* (Soho Theatre, 2007), *The Prophet* (Gate Theatre, 2012) and *Love, Bombs and Apples* (Arcola Theatre, 2016). He is the recipient of George Devine, Meyer-Whitworth and Pearson theatre awards as well as the Arab British Centre Award for Culture.

Anoud is an Iraqi-born author living in London.

Zhraa Alhaboby's writings incorporate history, mystery and medicine. She has published several novels in Arabic, including *The Sumerian Tales* series, set in ancient Mesopotamia 2500BC, and *Doves and Ravens*, which tackles inequality (both with Al-Hafez Publishing, Dubai, 2015). *When the Sun Escapes* (Al-Adeeb Publishing, Amman-Baghdad, 2008) visualises Babylon and Assyria around 750BC. Zhraa is a medical doctor and researcher, and studied International Primary Healthcare at the University of London.

Ali Bader was born in Baghdad, where he studied Western Philosophy and Foreign Literature, and now lives in Brussels. To date, he has published thirteen novels, several works of non-fiction, film scripts and plays, as well as two collections of poetry. He has also worked as a war correspondent covering the Middle East. His best-known novels include *Papa Sartre*, *The Tobacco Keeper*, *Running After Wolves*, and *The Sinful Woman*, all of which have won awards. He has written about art, politics and philosophy for many Arab newspapers and magazines.

Hassan Blasim was born in Baghdad in 1973, where he studied at the city's Academy of Cinematic Arts. In 1998, he was advised to leave Baghdad, as his documentary critiques of life under Saddam had put him at risk. He fled to Sulaymaniya (Iraqi Kurdistan), where he continued to make films, including the feature-length drama *Wounded Camera,* under the Kurdish pseudonym 'Ouazad Osman'. In 2004, after years of travelling illegally through Europe as a refugee, he finally settled in Finland. His first story to appear in print was for Comma's anthology *Madinah* (2008), edited by Joumana Haddad, which was followed by two commissioned collections, *The Madman of Freedom Square* (2009) and *The Iraqi Christ* (2013) – all translated into English by Jonathan Wright. The latter collection won the 2014 Independent Foreign Fiction Prize, and Hassan's stories have now been published in over 20 languages.

Mortada Gzar is an Iraqi novelist, filmmaker, and visual artist. Born in Kuwait in 1982, he has an engineering degree from the University of Baghdad, and has been a participant of the Iowa Writers' Workshop. He has written, directed and produced a number of films that have screened at international festivals. His animation 'Language' won the Doha Film Award. He is the author of three novels: *Broom of Paradise* (2008), *Sayyid Asghar Akbar* (2013), and *My Beautiful Cult* (2016), and is a regular contributor to the Lebanese newspaper *al-Safir al-Arabiandis.*

Jalal Hasan was born in Baghdad in 1968. He published his first story 'Five Travelers by Five Paper Boats' whilst still in secondary school and graduated from the University of Baghdad's Spanish Department in 1994. In 1992, after the publication of his 98-word story, 'The Last Day for Rain!' in the Lebanese Magazine *Al-Aadab*, Hasan was arrested and detained for seven months. After continued pressure on him personally, Hasan fled to Jordan in May 1997, and worked in Amman as a freelance writer and journalist, until he moved again to Arizona State, as a refugee in 1999. He currently lives with his wife and two children in Los Angeles, where he writes and drives a cab (what he calls 'the best job in the world!'). He has published two collections of short stories *The Last Day for Rain!* (1998) and *Meanwhile...in Baghdad* (2008, both with Alwah, Madrid). He is currently writing a novel.

Khalid Kaki was born in Kirkuk in 1971. He studied Spanish Literature and Philology at the University of Baghdad 1989–93, and at Autónoma University in Madrid (1997–2000) where he has lived since 1996. He has published four collections of poetry – *Unsafely* (Alwah, Madrid, 1998), *The Guard's Notes* (Alaliph, Madrid, 2001), *Cages in a Bird* (Phenix, Cairo 2005) and *Ashes of the Pomegranate Tree* (Alfalfa, Madrid, 2011) – and two collections of short stories – *The Land of Facing Mirrors* (Alahlia Editions, Baghdad 2005), and *The Suicide of Jose Buenavida* (Almutawasit, Milan 2016).

Diaa Jubaili was born in 1977 and still lives in Basra. Growing up he was unable to complete his education due to war and the economic blockade during the 90's. He is the author of five novels – *The Curse of the Marquis* (2007), which won the Dubai Magazine Award, *The Ugly face of Vincent* (2009), *Bogeys, the Bizarre* (2011), *General Stanley Maude's Souvenir* (2014) and *The Lion of Basra* (2016).

Ibrahim Al-Marashi is Associate Professor of History at California State University San Marcos. He is both a US and UK national, and obtained his doctorate from the University of Oxford, completing a thesis on the Iraqi invasion of Kuwait, part of which was plagiarised by the British government's 'Dodgy Dossier'. He is co-author of *Iraq's Armed Forces: An Analytical History* (Routledge, 2008), and *The Modern History of Iraq*, with Phebe Marr (Westview 2016).

About the Translators

Emre Bennett is a keen linguist and a fanatic reader of Middle-Eastern literature. He is an Arabic language graduate from the University of Westminster where he is currently studying a masters in Specialised Translation. He recently completed the City University's 'Translate the City' summer course in literary translation with Ruth Ahmedzai Kemp, and currently works part time as a translator and English tutor.

Katharine Halls's co-translation (with Adam Talib) of Raja Alem's prize-winning *The Dove's Necklace* appeared in 2016. Her film translations include Jasmina Metwaly and Philip Rizk's *Out On The Street* and Eyal Sivan's *Common State, Potential Conversation*, and her stage translations have been performed in Europe and the Middle East.

Elisabeth Jaquette is a writer and translator. Her translations of Arabic literature have been published in *Banipal* and Words Without Borders, and are forthcoming in *Portal 9*. She has worked as a translator for the PEN World Voices Festival, and has previously translated Rania Mamoun for *The Book of Khartoum* (Comma, 2016). Jaquette was a CASA fellow at the American University in Cairo in 2012–13, and is currently a graduate student at Columbia University.

Andrew Leber is a translator and researcher based in Doha. He graduated from Brown University and was a Fellow of the

Center for Arabic Study Abroad in Cairo from 2012 to 2013. He has previously translated short excerpts of Syrian and Palestinian literature, including a selection of Hani al-Rahib's *The Epidemic* (1981), Saadallah Wanous' play *The Elephant, Your Majesty* (1969), along with an assortment of writings by Gazan authors Najlaa Ataallah and Atef Abu Saif.

Adam Talib is the translator of Fadi Azzam's *Sarmada*, Khairy Shalaby's *The Hashish Waiter*, and Mekkawi Said's *Cairo Swan Song*. Most recently he co-translated (with Katharine Halls) Raja Alem's *The Dove's Necklace*. He teaches classical Arabic literature at the American University in Cairo.

Max Weiss is Elias Boudinot Bicentennial Preceptor and Assistant Professor of History and Near Eastern Studies at Princeton University. He is the author of *In the Shadow of Sectarianism: Law, Shi`ism, and the Making of Modern Lebanon*, and the translator from the Arabic of Samar Yazbek, *A Woman in the Crossfire: Diaries of the Syrian Revolution*, and Nihad Sirees, *The Silence and the Roar*. Currently he is translating Mamdouh Azzam, *Ascension to Death*.

Jonathan Wright is a British journalist and literary translator. He joined Reuters news agency in 1980 as a correspondent, and has been based in the Middle East for most of the last three decades. He has served as Reuters' Cairo bureau chief, and he has lived and worked throughout the region, including in Egypt, Sudan, Lebanon, Tunisia and the Gulf. From 1998 to 2003, he was based in Washington, DC, covering U.S. foreign policy for Reuters. For two years until the fall of 2011 Wright was editor of the *Arab Media & Society Journal*, published by the Kamal Adham Center for Journalism Training and Research at the American University in Cairo. He is the translator of all of Hassan Blasim's fiction in English.

Special Thanks

The publishers would like to thank Christine Gilmore, Chelsea Milsom, Lauren Pyott and Noor Hemani, all of whom worked as editorial assistants at various points on this project, as well as CASAW (the Centre for the Advanced Study of the Arabic World), English Pen and The British Institute for the Study of Iraq, who supported the project financially. Particular thanks are also due to Lauren Mulvee and Erica Jarnes for their patience and support throughout.